TODAY & TOMORROW

A NOVEL BY
OFELIA HUNT

Mᴀɢɪᴄ ❄ Hᴇʟɪᴄᴏᴘᴛᴇʀ Pʀᴇss
Northampton, MA
May 2011

TODAY

ONE

One birthday-card had a penguin standing atop a glacier, the sky dark behind it. I set it on the coffee table. I surveyed my apartment, the high windows and empty white walls. I opened all the blinds on all the windows and turned off my television. I said to the television, "I'll never turn you on again." I apologized. "Really sorry about this. Probably I'll watch you sometime, nostalgically, but can't watch you so much anymore because I'm twenty years-old and it's time to grow up and adults listen only to AM radio—to NPR, Morning Edition or whatever, or ESPN—so I'm going to listen to NPR a lot and feel sort of intellectual or liberal I think, or maybe progressive. I'm not sure which is which yet..." The television didn't answer and I was saddened by the television's silence but then relieved. Now I'm lying on my brown leather loveseat and there's sun outside and the sun's sunlight's in my apartment and I can see little bits of dust moving and interacting with other dust-bits and it's warm and comfortable even though it's December.

I'm twenty-years-old today. This is very important. I told my boyfriend before he left on his bicycle for work. I vacuumed our apartment. I loaded, then emptied the dishwasher. I filed away the birthday-cards I'd left to be filed away.

I want to be naked on my loveseat in the sunlight but Ron, my neighbor, would call the police or masturbate quickly on his deck. Print pornographic leaflets, place them in mailboxes, on the club-house bulletin-board, maybe taped carefully to each apartment-door. Think then that I'm ugly or alien somehow—photograph the naked me, show the photographs at dinner-parties over Cosmopolitans or White-Russians. Ron's leaning over his railing. He's wearing a red and gray striped sweater and I imagine the striped sweater unraveling slowly and burning quietly alone on the deck, and his wife emerging from the apartment, frightened, saying, "What the fuck? What the fuck?" and Ron's shoulder-shrug then, or mustached smile. I roll over and take my cell-phone from the coffee-table and begin a text-message. I type, 'There are twenty-seven tangents in the tangent-room.' I send this to my boyfriend, Erik. Ron's sitting on his little deck with his legs spread, picking at the inseam of his corduroy pants. I wonder if Ron's thinking about my naked body, or simply my nipples. I imagine Ron sitting with Erik discussing my nipples. There are sketches, diagrams. Three-color prints, auto-cad designs. A laser-pointer and a PowerPoint. An overhead-projector. Ron's wife waving her hands affirmatively, then grabbing slowly her own wide breast. I compose another text-message. I type, 'There are twenty-seven tangerines in the tangerine-room.' I send this to Erik.

I decide slowly to call my sister Merna. I won't know what to say. We haven't spoken in four years. It's been sad and barren, a kind of long white hallway with buzzing fluorescent lights. Un-ringing telephones on beat-up nightstands. Telephone-books stacked crookedly in front of empty apartments. Maybe it was sad and barren for only a few months, then became embarrassing. Now it must be sad and barren again, on my birthday, and I think I should call Merna, arrange a meeting, because it'll be talkshow-like, soft gray sofas, organ-music, fuzzy camera-filters, monologues with a vengeful backbeat. I've never known how to talk to my sister. I was at her house once. I said, "Your kitten's so pretty I could just pull her eyes out and roll them along the kitchen floor." Merna laughed quietly. The kitten was a black little ball. "I love your kitten," I said. I lifted the kitten by her scruff, and stroked the kitten in my arms until it purred. "Kitten-eye marbles," I said. Merna began unloading her dishwasher. The plates were white and clean with the tiniest bubbles of water huddling away from her rag and my sister was merciless as she carefully wiped every part of every plate and obliterated each tiny perfect bubble and slowly set each plate in its proper stack in the cupboard next to the refrigerator. I hated her plates then, her bubble-obliterating rag, her stupid silly kitten. The plates clinked as she stacked them and I wanted to clink that way. She was lovely and it seemed peaceful and quiet and I could even, at that moment, imagine days of lovely waiting in the kitchen, drying dishes, stacking them in cupboards, lining cupboard-shelves with rose-scented shelf-paper. Building new cupboards then, filling them with plastic Wal-Mart dishes. I whispered something but I can't remember what. Merna finished drying the plates. I held the kitten carefully in one hand. Merna sat across from me and stared at my hands in a puzzling way and began to braid her long brown hair. Outside, the sky was a thin gray puff, very large and nearby. I cocked the kitten. The kitten was heavy. The kitten was cocked and I flung it and it moved slowly, sprawl-legged toward the window and the window shivered in anticipation and Merna and I gasped and there was a loud sound I can't describe but was both wonderful and terrible and the kitten bounced and moved slowly toward the sink, its tiny legs stretched out oddly, at angles, as though disconnected from its round furry body.

TWO

I think I've torn my quadriceps.

I stand, circle my coffee-table, test my quadriceps. I stretch, pull off my blue-jeans and examine my quadriceps, massage them gently with my hands. "It's okay," I say. "I'm sorry," I say. I imagine my quadriceps healthy, un-torn. Blood-cells moving through them carrying vital molecules that mend the quadriceps-tear, the multiple tears which must radiate from the initial wound. I open my cell-phone address book and select my boyfriend's name. My boyfriend's name is Todd.

"Hi Erik," I say into my cell-phone. Sometimes I call Todd Erik.

"My name's not Erik," Erik says.

"I'm sorry Erik."

"My name's Todd," Erik says.

"I know. Forget about that. It's my birthday and I tore my quadriceps. So what are we doing tonight? Robbing Wells Fargo, then escape to Mexico and hide from the FBI, the CIA maybe, live there in the desert with horses and orange groves?" Erik doesn't answer. "Hijack jetplanes, fly to the South Pacific or something where we can lay secretly on the beach, make quiet cell-phone calls to our families?"

"I have to work, okay. I'm working now. I'll call you later, maybe." Erik turns off his cell-phone. Erik once told me we could live in New

Mexico. "It's warmer there," he said. "We'll just camp out. Live in a van or something, in a parking-lot. We can be those people who sell flags in parking-lots. We'll get a big-top tent." I select a long gray skirt and a t-shirt from my closet. I iron my skirt and t-shirt. I wonder where we'd get the flags. What kind of flags? Would we design them ourselves? Does Erik know how to sew? I put on the ironed skirt and t-shirt and put my iron away. I want to ask Erik about the flags. I want a Jolly-Roger. We could dress only in eye-patches. I drive my little Honda to Wal-Mart where Erik works in his little blue vest. I wonder if all parking-lots are really one parking-lot. It's possible. You could start in Boise, at the mall, and move carefully to New Mexico in a few minutes.

"Where's Erik?" I say to the cashier.

"Huh?"

"Erik's the regional exploitation manager, charged with destroying unions before they form."

"Oh."

"Like a parasite, kind of. A human-sized tape-worm. He's from New Mexico or something."

"I don't think I've seen him before."

"Have you ever seen a tape-worm?" I look carefully at the cashier's blue vest. It's very crisp and clean and I want suddenly to touch the vest, to reach forward and run my finger along the vest-edge, to unbutton the vest and remove the vest and wear the vest myself. I want suddenly to be this cashier and to wear her blue vest and scan barcodes, take payment, cash only, make change, carefully counted back, the coins burnished until they shine, the cash laundered and dried somehow so it remains crisp and

6

new. The cashier's nametag says 'Julia'. "You're very pretty Julia," I say. "People watch you carefully and say to themselves 'Julia's very pretty' and walk through Wal-Mart and buy things thinking only of the pretty Julia. Right? Isn't that right."

"Hmm," Julia says. "Hmm." Julia turns away.

"Don't go," I say. "It's my birthday, and I tore my quadriceps but I'm strong and I'm going to get through."

"Get through," Julia says, her body perpendicular to mine.

"Yes, I'm going to get through and I'm here and I want to buy things, like five cart-loads of 30 weight oil, and to find Erik. Do you know Erik?"

"I have to work," Julia says, swinging her head side to side. "I'm working, okay."

"But I want to buy things."

Julia drifts slowly toward her cash register. Julia's arms are puffy and pale and Julia's arms move separately from Julia's body and I love them and want Julia's arms. I want to remove Julia's arms and place them on my body and wear them like I'm Julia and like Julia's arms are my arms. I walk toward the toy section. I walk as though I'm wearing Julia's arms. All my parts move separately. Erik's bent over near the Hot Wheels. He's tall and pale and very thin and his hair's a tangled brown mess. Erik's eyes are clear and flat, his face blank. His hands and long thin fingers move quickly and precisely, arranging remote-control dune-buggies on a white perforated shelf and then carded stock-car Hot Wheels onto poke-outs. Fluorescent-light-panels light the toys, the floor, even the shelves very evenly and it's amazing to be everywhere surrounded by fluorescent-light. I whisper to myself, "Erik is Todd, Erik is Todd." Erik looks up.

"Erik," I say. "Fluorescent light-panels."

"My name's Todd."

"Couldn't I call you Erik for a while? Would that be so bad?"

"I don't know."

I met Erik while robbing an AM/PM. I was using a butterfly-knife. I use butterfly-knives when I rob AM/PMs. I said to the clerk, "Give me your fucking money." I showed him my butterfly-knife. "AM/PM?" I ask Erik.

"What are you talking about?"

"Don't know," I say. "It's my birthday." Erik continues to arrange toys—now G.I. Joes, Teenage Mutant Ninja Turtles, Storm Troopers. His fingers move rigidly and the toys form geometric ranks, some into simple squares and rectangles, others into bright parallelograms or hexagons, little battalions maybe, formations Erik has designed instantaneously and I wonder why Erik has formed them in this way. "This is good work. It's very beautiful." Erik moves down the aisle and straightens his blue vest. I pull a small G.I. Joe from the shelf. "I'll take this doll from its package."

"It's not a doll." Erik moves further down the aisle.

"I'll do it."

I tear the packaging and think about stacks of green cardboard, bales of it, giant cardboard walls, in Memphis maybe, or Seattle, tiny G.I. Joe replicas manning the battlements. A solitary flag, Erik on a field of green. There are instructions and an accessory-list—rope, AK47, other things. I crinkle the plastic covering. I love this G.I. Joe. What kind of flags would G.I. Joe carry? It's small and muscular and everything's green. The arms and legs move smoothly. There's an eye-patch and I can position the arms and legs however I choose. I position the G.I. Joe in a diving motion, then carefully throw it as if throwing a dart. It moves missile-like through the air, deadly somehow, a green army-wasp. It strikes Erik's shoulder, tumbles sideways to the floor. Erik moves further down the aisle, his face flat and calm. G.I. Joe retains his diving form on the linoleum. I move terribly close to Erik. I taste Erik's air and it's sour and I breathe Erik's air until we share the same air, until the air's suffocating and warm.

"Go away," Erik says. "I'm working. I'm straightening the aisle. I have to straighten this aisle and the next aisle and the next aisle until I have straightened all aisles. There are probably a million aisles. I have to keep going until every aisle's straightened. Can't you see that?" Erik swings his arm around. "These aisles are full of little disorders and sometimes little empty people, graham-crackers, empty animal-cracker boxes, circus-car shaped—Barnum's Animals, you know, in little cages. I have to straighten each aisle until all aisles are straightened." Erik moves slowly away from me. Everything's lighted at the same level from every angle. There are no shadows. I push plastic horses to the floor, some carrying armored knights. All the horses are evenly lighted and shadow-less. I move toward Erik but he's organizing very quickly and moving from aisle to aisle and the Wal-Mart's full of so many people and these people block my path with their shopping carts and each person looks like every other person but larger somehow than the person before and I become confused. I squat near a DVD-spinner. Bill Murray stares at me and he's beautiful there in a striped shirt and a dark suit, holding firmly a bouquet of roses. Bill Murray's the opposite of me. I want slowly to hold his withered eyes. I shove Bill Murray in my skirt and walk carefully toward the exit. My arms and legs tense and seem about to shake but I concentrate and hold them still. I imagine the arm and leg muscles, stretched and tightened, gripping at each end my bones. I look at Julia. I wave. Julia stares away from me and straightens her blue vest, each hand straightening a different part of the vest. Thousands of people stand in hundreds of lines and wait to scan cart-loads of Pepsi or gallons of milk, tater-tots, little fleece blankets, and the thousands are almost identical, each person larger somehow than the person before. I imagine each person staring impersonally at me, noting anthropological markers. My hips maybe, or my spine, the scoliosis there, or some incongruity in my face, the shallow scar above my left eye. I'm about to shake violently so I feel Bill Murray in my skirt and love Bill Murray because Bill Murray's not shaking. Bill Murray's solid and immobile. I think the words: I love I love I love... I step through the sliding door and feel a terrible feeling and quicken my legs until I'm outside. There's a beeping but I focus on forward movement and in a moment I'm sitting in my little Honda, driving my little Honda slowly away.

THREE

If I could love every moving thing, I would donate to NPR, become a member, urge Merna to donate, or Erik, would campaign for NPR, steal NPR, make it my own. A moment ago the stoplight turned green. I sat very still and watched my dashboard digital-clock until the light turned red. I listened to NPR and learned about the thriving city of Karachi, its newly developed beaches and golf courses, then was asked by NPR to donate. Now dozens of sedans have lined up behind me. Steam rises from their hoods and the hoods and sedans are all a dull gray and the same model—some kind of Toyota, a Camry maybe, Corolla? In my rearview mirror I can see the people in the cars, white-knuckled hands on steering-wheels. There's snow on roofs, gray and dirty. I think about steering-wheels, hairy hands with long segmented fingers. The finger-movements then. I want to be the people who donate. I hear a horn and imagine drivers disintegrating slowly, their cars disintegrating, the road dark and empty except for the thin layer of ash. Ash-donations. Could we sort the ash genetically? Return it in white satin packages to its ash-families? Dust slowly lining the New Mexico desert. The light turns green. What would Bill Murray do? I depress the gas-pedal. I consider Bill Murray. The beauty of Bill Murray. The craggy lined face of Bill Murray. Bill Murray puppet in my pocket. I imagine Bill Murray strolling languidly along snow-covered sidewalks, his hands in fists, punching leafless cherry-trees. The trees fall over—Bill Murray crying carefully in the snow. I park my little Honda in the McDonald's parking-lot and turn it off. The parking-lot's wide with white rectangular slots and surrounded on all sides by rounded curbs. I say, "A grid, a grid grid." NPR wants me to donate. I can donate at any level. Bill Murray doesn't park in parking-lots or donate to NPR. If I were sitting in my little Honda with Erik, we might hold hands. Erik might slowly massage my quadriceps, offer to go into McDonald's, rob the McDonald's, take for us a bag of french fries, bags of french fries, our own salt-shaker, a tub of catsup. We could escape then, to Astoria maybe, or Seattle. We could make our own grids, our own french fries.

The cashier's not Erik. He's thin and lanky with little red pimples. He has no nametag. He seems suddenly about to scratch but doesn't scratch so I only imagine him slowly scratching. Everyone should have a nametag. I decide to make my own nametag. To make an Erik nametag, pin it to his chest. Flag-shaped. Flags arranged in parking-spaces. The business opportunity of the century. Erik and I in New Mexico wearing only eye-patches. Jolly-Rogers. Nametags pinned to our nipples. "Where is everyone?" I ask. "Don't you need cooks or whatever? What about the drive-through? Who's operating the drive-thru?"

"Robots, I'd say. We've automated it—probably it's automated." He stares at me with little green eyes. Erik has little black eyes, I think. Erik doesn't have eyes. "I'm lying about that. Sorry, I think I'm funny. My friends say I think I'm funny, so—" he says. "Everybody's breaking or—I'll probably be okay. Smoking. People could be smoking. I've never run the store by myself, but I'm okay, probably, as long as no one orders the fish-sandwich. If it were automated, it'd be better. I could monitor automated-robots probably, if someone trained me, even with fish-sandwiches or remote-controls, some kind of teleprompter."

"You'll be okay. Do you like animals?" I look at his little green eyes. I want desperately to ask the boy why I said that. "Why'd I say that?"

"I don't know—I don't think."

"Wait, which question are you answering?"

"Both questions, I think," he says. "I've been trained to multitask and I think animals are nice sometimes or at least to see animals on television, brightly and from a distance. Probably animals on television are good and tame, and I have a cat and a betta fish which I like, but if my fish or my cat were electrocuted, or decapitated, I probably wouldn't be sad or anything, or—animals are probably like anything else, at least, you know, I wouldn't be sad if I broke my television or whatever. I'd just get a new television, maybe high-definition, a better one, something."

I trace his hand to his wrist. Does Erik have a wrist? The hand and wrist are hairy but the hair's smooth and soft and each hair's thin and softly curled so that at my touch the hairs tangle then untangle. Erik decapitating a betta fish. Bill Murray. "Soft hair," I say. I tell myself to not say thoughts then wonder what I mean.

"Want a hamburger or something? You could have an extra-value-meal. I like extra-value-meals. There's one with fish. Chicken-nuggets, chicken-patties. With hamburgers. There are pictures up there. Safety in extra-value-meals, I think, probably, because they're orderly, with pictures, and—" I sit on the floor, cross-legged. The tiles are cool and flat. I lean against the thick metal railing and consider the menu. The cashier's little green eyes focus on me then the ceiling. He wipes the counter in a circular motion with a rag he pulls from his back pocket. The circles expand and contract and the rag's very damp and thin and his hands are moving the rag delicately and I think how it's beautiful, beautiful and how I want to move the rag that way, to hold the rag in my hand, soft and damp, moving so circularly. I want something. I think about wanting.

"When I threw the kitten," I say, "It bounced around." The cashier pulls off his hat and combs his hair with his long fingers and the long fingers move slowly through the hair and the hair springs up in a sudden way and the hair's very black and shiny and it springs blackly and the light from the ceiling lights the hair and all the hair and light and everything overwhelm me so I lean against the railing until I can feel only the railing on my back. I breathe very deeply and stare at the floor and hope he's put his hat back on his very narrow head and covered his black and shiny hair. "You don't understand," I say. "I'm like a serial-killer. It starts with kittens." I look at the little green eyes and they look back at me. "It starts with kittens, then it's everything—you think about strangling constantly, like right now I'm imagining stabbing your neck, two, three times, both sides maybe. I can see the knife, a switch-blade, in your neck and the blood moving along the counter then your co-workers rushing around you, removing the knife, but it's too late and you're lying on the floor. Your little green eyes are wide open and moving side to side jerkily and somebody's using your little rag to wipe your blood in little circles and your long fingers are reaching for the rag but they can't reach the rag.

That's how it is. You know, with kittens." I stop. "And you can't reach the rag," I say again. I watch the boy for a while. He holds his rag. "I'll take some chicken-nuggets." The boy brings the nuggets. They're in a little cardboard-box with air-holes as though little nuggets need to breathe.

"You can have those for free," the boy says. "No one'll say anything."

"I probably wouldn't stab you."

"Thanks. I appreciate that. I really do."

I try to say something new but can't so I take the nuggets in the little chicken-nugget-box, making certain my hands don't cover the air-holes. I think about chicken-nuggets in New Mexico, chicken-nuggets next to me in the parking-lot that is all parking-lots, Erik there, the cashier, our bodies covered with pink flags. "I'd take you home," I say. "Make dinner, help with homework, maybe, with mammals or thermodynamics or whatever." I walk outside. It's dark with a thousand clouds that are one cloud and probably it's going to rain or snow soon and the cars will roll slowly and there will be a loud hissing everywhere and it will be pleasant like television static, like other things, like my hand on a sweater. I hear my cell-phone ring-tone, pull my cell-phone from my pocket, open it. It's Merna. I don't know what to say to Merna. She says something about my birthday. It starts with kittens. I don't answer and I don't even breathe because I'm afraid Merna will hear me and if Merna hears me, Merna will expect me to say something about kittens and I can't talk to Merna in front of McDonald's holding carefully my chicken-nuggets. Kitten-nuggets. I think of the sky as one cloud and wonder if there's only one nugget, if all chicken-nuggets are connected, individual cells of one super-nugget organism—like Voltron.

I close my cell-phone. A man's pushing an empty shopping-cart. He's very old and has long gray hair and a beard. His green coat has many pockets that seem all at once useful and yet I wonder what a person could use all those pockets for. It's a lovely coat and I want so much to have a coat just like it with many pockets and I would even think for a while and fill each pocket carefully. I picture fishhooks in the pockets and crumbs, then the crumbs growing slowly or sorted by type, by molecule, then combining somehow into stiff dry meals. Lay the coat in a summer garden and watch as tomatoes and corn stalks sprout from the pockets. I hold out my chicken-nuggets in their little chicken-nugget-box with air-holes. "Take them," I say to the old man. The old man looks at me in a small way and I hold the chicken-nuggets near his face and he looks at the chicken-nuggets in the same small way and his eyes become round and tired. "Don't worry," I say, "they're dead." I look at the very old man and his round and tired eyes. "They won't hurt anyone anymore."

FOUR

I walk along the sidewalk next to the highway. My car's somewhere. Everything's graph-paper. The highway's six lanes, three north, three south, and in each lane are hundreds of gray sedans with halogen headlights and antennas and each sedan moves in its own vector, some wobbling along a kind of axis and others zooming very straight and even the speeds vary and it's tremendous how each sedan can move so separately in similar vectors—a person would have to be crazy to drive with so many people, with so many sedans and lanes. There are hundreds of Douglas-firs planted along the sidewalk. I consider mountain-climbing slowly toward a distant parking-lot. Parking-lots like terraces stepping up Mount Rainier. Fresh asphalt, flat and level, snow and sun above. I tightly hug my body but there's wind and I continue to shiver. Behind me a fat man adjusts his puffy black rain-parka. He's very fat with blond hair and he walks swiftly. When he sees me watching he slows. I stare fixedly at my cell-phone, push buttons as though entering a text-message. When I look over my shoulder again he's striding swiftly toward me. He slows, whistles, watches the passing sedans. He's very near now, whistling bird-calls.

I turn and stare at his chin. I say, "What do you want?"

He looks at me with a wide mouth and funny big eyes. "Me?" He watches me and the eyes move like little black rocks in his face.

I feel distracted and look at the clouds which are only one cloud, then back at him. He has drawn nearer somehow. "I'm just paranoid, probably just paranoid," I say quietly to myself as I eye the width of his elongated shadow. I can almost feel his puffy black rain-parka, the wet plastic bulges of it like restrained flesh. His head's tiny and his face is not even a little chubby, and it seems the face is missing flesh which I search for but can't find.

"Coffee?" He licks his lower lip very slowly. His tongue's small and quick and he only uses the tip to lick his lower lip and it's strange how slowly the tongue moves when the tongue's very small and quick and pink. I stare with little eyes at the tongue and feel as though it's staring back, recording, analyzing somehow my face. "You don't remember me?" he asks. "We could get espresso. I know this place with a thousand coffees. Aromatic specialties, Bolivian roasts, everything. I'd even pay. We'll discuss our past associations. You still drive your little Honda?" He waits for my nod. "You see, we're old friends. We'll talk at this café. I have information, and you'll want this information, trust me. It's cold out here and this café's very cozy, with upholstered chairs, great lighting."

"You know my boyfriend or something?"

"I don't think so."

"It's my birthday today. Today, I'm twenty."

"Lisbon must be beautiful this time of year."

I feel a sudden panic in my legs. "How do I know you?" I ask. "Seriously?"

"We met in New Mexico," he says. He opens the café door.

The café's warm. There are brown corduroy sofas and dark chandeliers with soft light-bulbs that hang at different levels and project long bulbous shadows around my feet. He tells me his name's Aaron. Aaron's in the bathroom and I'm sitting on a corduroy sofa, sipping bitter coffee, moving my feet between the long bulbous shadows—and though the café's almost empty, I feel as though I'm watched, like the watchers are whispering about kittens and arson. I can almost hear something like, "Her clothes aren't at all stylish," and "Her cheeks are very large, the forehead seems to sort of protrude, doesn't it? Sort of potato-like." But when I look around I don't see anyone, not even the barista. Aaron returns. He removes his black and puffy rain-parka and carefully lays it on the sofa-arm. As he sinks into the sofa the far ends of two brown cushions rise slowly, almost curling. My cell-phone ring-tone plays a little song. It's Erik. "I'm sorry," I say. "Just a moment." I open my cell-phone. "Yes?"

"What're you doing right now?" Erik asks.

"Right now?"

Aaron shrugs and looks out the window and then crosses his arms and sighs, his lips pursing, frowning. Aaron has very narrow shoulders and I can see them move beneath his sweater.

"Come home. I need you right now, to strip naked and lay on the couch, with your tongue, think about me and I want you to reach with your hand op—"

"Aren't you working?"

"I need you to touch down there."

I wonder if Aaron can hear then look down between the long shadows. "I have to go," I whisper.

"And I want your puss—"

I close my cell-phone and watch my feet and put my cell-phone away and think about touching myself and look at Aaron. "I'm very sorry about that," I mumble.

"It's nothing. Don't think about it. Think about Lisbon."

"What?"

"Lisbon, in Portugal. Your birthday present."

"Yes." I look at my hands and my fingernails and compare my fingernails and wonder why each fingernail's not identical. Aaron's also looking at my fingernails and he's smiling widely and his very narrow face is sort of slack and tired.

"You said you had information." I feel as though I've lost something in mentioning this, and Aaron's moving closer, his face no longer tired but narrow and broad and wide and smiling and he has many teeth and each tooth gives the impression of smiling and there are a thousand gaps between the teeth and I watch the gaps and turn from the gaps and the gaps between Aaron's teeth are very parallel. I touch the edge of the tabletop and run my finger along it and my finger feels the edge and I'm feeling my finger feel the edge of the tabletop.

"Information," Aaron says. "Could be opportunity. I don't know."

"I'm going to Lisbon," I say. "You don't think I'm going to Lisbon but I'm going to Lisbon."

"Of course you are. Don't worry about that. Let me show you something." With his wide chubby hand, Aaron reaches into his pocket.

His eyes are like little black rocks. They could be Erik's eyes if Erik had eyes. Aaron reaches across the tabletop, his hand fisted, and slowly, as the hand moves toward me, opens the hand. There's a money-clip, a quarter-inch thick with hundreds folded flatly. He shoves it toward me. "For you," Aaron says. "Take it."

"What?"

"You're hired." Aaron leans back and the couch slides a little. "You can be my assistant, you know, assist me."

"How?"

Aaron smiles his wide smile and turns his hand in an upward twirling gesture. "This and that. Everybody needs money," he says. "I'll take you to Lisbon, if you want—I'll take you to Lisbon to the beach and you'll walk with me along the bright sand near little waves and we'll be naked there and lie in the sand and let the sand get on our bodies, in Lisbon. Beautiful, right? Everyone needs a little money. You know. An arrangement." Outside, a boy and a girl are walking slowly and looking inside the café window. "You're very pretty," Aaron says.

The boy brushes his hair back and touches the girl's shoulder in a slow way.

"Have you ever decapitated a kitten?" I say.

"Why would I?"

"Sometimes I want to stab kitten-faces, you know, with a kitchen-knife. I'd stab the kittens and decapitate them and throw the little kitten-heads out the window, or maybe save and dry the heads and make little kitten-head-dolls for my mantle, if I had a mantle."

"What do you mean?"

Aaron's reflection sits lightly in the window, expanded and rippled somehow, his striped seaman's sweater mottling the boy and girl until they disappear.

"I'm tired. I'm tired of kittens, tired of things like that. Let's rob the café. I have a knife. We'll rob the café, kill the barista and take the tip-jar. I want that goddamn tip-jar."

"Sshh," Aaron says, glaring wildly around. "Don't say things like that out loud."

"I'll say whatever I want. I'm your assistant, right. It's the arrangement. I say whatever I want."

Aaron grunts and leans back and smiles a tired smile.

My cell-phone ring-tone plays a little song.

"I'm sorry," I say. It's Erik again. I open my cell-phone. "What?" I say.

Erik's panting. "I'm sorry about before," he says. "You're just so fucking hot. I want your naked titties and your legs all spread your hand, your hand there—"

"I'm busy right now," I say. "I'm having coffee with Aaron. We're talking about kittens."

I turn off my cell-phone.

"Let's rob an AM/PM," I say. "I want a Pepsi."

FIVE

"I had two sisters but I killed Anastasia accidentally. We were swimming in this little pond—my parents took us to this shack in the woods and there was a pond there and the pond was very dark and reflective. Anyway, Anastasia and Merna, that's my older sister, were swimming in the pond and it was cold, because it was winter, and, Merna's the oldest, I'm the middle, and we're racing from one end of the pond to the other. We're all naked, I was fourteen, and suddenly I'm very tall and I'm swimming and I'm winning and I'm watching the pond-edge and the dirt and the dirty little rocks and I'm swimming very fast—my arms feel long and Merna's saying 'bitch,' and then 'you bitch,' and I stop. I'm at the edge. Merna's wild and angry and Anastasia's in front of me and we're all crazy then. There was this movement, this shaking in us and I could feel something there—like hydrogen peroxide maybe. I can't explain it but it was solid somehow. Anastasia's there in front of me and I see it in her. So I grab a rock from the pond-edge, smash one eye then another and grab Anastasia's hair and hold her there beneath the dirty pond-water. It was an accident, I think. Merna was very angry and I was afraid of a thousand things and I smashed her with a rock and held her beneath the pond-water."

"You're lying," Aaron says. "I don't believe anything."

We're in my apartment. Aaron has sprawled his pudgy oversized body on my loveseat. He's leaning very backward and rolling his blond hair on the sofa-back. It waves there. It ripples and flattens in a glittering way. Aaron's long arms cover the sofa-top and his very large very thin hands grasp the sofa-corners, each finger splayed out, separated, index fingers rubbing slowly the sofa-edge. Earlier I moved my coffee-table into the kitchen and now I'm pacing in front of Aaron. His little eyes follow me like dense black rocks and it's like night outside though it's hardly noon and the day seems all at once a useless and boring thing.

"Merna's so lovely," I say. "You should see her photo, pre-disfigurement."

"Disfigurement?"

"Mother stabbed her face two or three times, slashed at her nose, her cheeks." I drag my finger down my cheek in demonstration. "Said she was 'correcting mistakes.' Ten years ago, I think. Family-reunion. Dad was gone then. He was a merchant-marine or something. Mom was screaming. We were at this beach-park, Golden Gardens. It was a barbeque."

"Hmm." Aaron yawns.

"Let's talk about something else," I say. "Let's talk about global-terrorism, or fashion-design. Do you like fashion? Do you think I'm fashionable?" Aaron slowly removes his arms from the couch and rolls them carefully toward his body. The arms touch Aaron's chest and slide smoothly toward his lap and rest there in an agonizing way. The hands and fingers skitter like little ants toward Aaron's knees where they become taut and solid, fixed points on a three-dimensional grid. I'm

24

moving, I think, I'm not moving. "I feel a little crazy today," I say. "Am I fashionable? I don't know. I want to be a little fashionable."

"You're fashionable enough. You're very pretty."

"I kind of want to be a terrorist. Terrorists are terribly fashionable."

"Oh, hmm?"

"Maybe it's just fashionable to hate terrorists or something," I say. "I'm a liar. I don't want to be a terrorist today. I want to steal everything all at once and take it someplace safe, bury it. That's what I really want."

"Don't talk like that."

"I talk how I want. That's part of the arrangement."

The refrigerator has alphabet-magnets and beneath the alphabet-magnets are Erik's drawings and the drawings drawn by Erik, or Todd, are all crayon-y and round and with breasts and inflated penises and balloons and kittens and they're arranged on the refrigerator door in an aggressive way—each drawing covering another, at angles from every other drawing—and I'm frightened by the terrible organization of it. I can't open the refrigerator-door or even for one moment look away from the drawings. Erik has drawn these pictures for me. I know this. Why though, do I know this?

"What is it?"

"Nothing," I answer.

There's a click and the front door's opening.

It's Erik. Erik's not drawing but I know he could suddenly begin to draw. Pull crayons from his pockets, fall cross-legged to the kitchen-floor, sketch slowly a self-portrait on the linoleum. I'm looking at Erik's Adidas. He ordered them online and each night he wipes them clean with Windex and paper-towels. Adidas-drawing. The crisp white stripes will remain white. Adidas flags at half-mast in a windy Wal-Mart parking-lot, the big-top half-built, our thousand flags for sale, arranged on blankets, held down with little black rocks. Erik seems much taller and thinner than before. His little clear eyes focus and refocus around the apartment. "I'm home," he says. Erik's slouching, hands in jeans. He sees Aaron. "Who's this?" Aaron slowly stands. There's a sound like crinkling paper but louder and more agitated and Aaron's on his feet and Aaron's arms are long bulky triangles and Erik stands in front of him, his chin a pointy knot in his face. I stand between them. It makes me laugh, standing between them. I'm the middle, I think. I laugh. Middle-land.

"I'm Aaron," Aaron says.

"I'm Todd," Erik says.

"I'm Todd," I say, and laugh some more.

Aaron and Erik watch me, their faces expressionless. Their little clear eyes move only to blink and I blink and we're all blinking and it's painful to see the little clear eyes, the little clear breaths, to blink and see them and blink and see them again. I want suddenly to be alone, to sit on my sofa, to read or watch television, to listen to NPR, to think then about Lisbon and kittens. But it's only useless desire so I consider my refrigerator and the crayon-y Erik-drawings and Aaron's narrow hands and narrow face, Erik's brown mess of hair and the dirty pond-water and how I could at any moment hold Aaron and Erik beneath the dirty pond-water. Two nights ago I couldn't sleep and I left my bed and sat on the sofa. I imagined little clear eyes watching me and I read from Two Against One and then Harper's and still couldn't sleep, and reading, sitting there, even the outside window-dark was only painful and tiring, so I sat very still and stopped everything I had the power to stop. It's like that now, maybe. I could stop everything in a moment, if I concentrate.

"We should sit at the dining-room table."

"We don't have a dining-room," Erik says.

"Here," I say. I point. We sit. It's cold but I'm too tired to turn on the heat. At the dining-room table we're almost an equilateral triangle. "Erik, could you move to the left, maybe three inches?" Erik moves. Centered and equidistant from each of us is a People with a Bill Murray cover and Bill Murray's hair's thin and lanky and he's smiling but in a suspicious way, as though he knows someone's photographing him and he doesn't want to be photographed. His little hairy hand's holding a white plastic-bag. What's in the bag? I don't know. I could hold a white plastic-bag. Aaron and Erik look around, forcing their eyes to focus only on objects and Aaron shrugs a little and gazes at the ceiling and Erik taps the table. "It's my birthday, we should commit a terrorist-act." Aaron chuckles. "What's in the plastic-bag?" I ask. "Anthrax? I've always thought Bill Murray was a terrorist. It's very sexy. He could put anything in a bag. I think it's a baby."

"I quit my job," Erik says. "I don't work for Wal-Mart anymore. I turned in my name-badge. It was magnetic. Well-designed, I'd say. I liked the job, you know, but I straightened everything that could be straightened and there was nothing left to straighten or organize so I told my boss, I think his name's Jim, anyway I told Jim I was a waste of money. I've organized everything now. I reached the pinnacle or something."

"I wish I could stab something," I say. "Anthrax-bag."

Aaron turns the People over. "I couldn't stand it. Bill Murray was staring at me."

"We should go to the shopping-mall. We could have a portrait made of us, then steal one-thousand wood massage things, you know the wood things with the little wood balls." I cross my arms beneath my breasts and wonder if Erik's staring at the breasts. He's told me he can detect nipples at one hundred feet. Sometimes he grabs my breasts when we're alone, watching TV maybe, on the loveseat, his thin fingers suddenly there, on my nipples.

"Has beady eyes, Bill Murray. Can't stand him staring at me. Feels wrong."

Erik turns to Aaron. "Have you ever been to Wal-Mart? Do you know how big it is, how full? I organized fucking everything."

SIX

We're at the shopping-mall surrounded by blue and gray floor-tiles arranged in concentric squares, blue surrounding gray surrounding blue.

"Seriously Aaron," Erik says. "Are you trying to fuck my girlfriend?"

"I don't fuck."

"It's all fucking," I say.

The ceiling's high and rounded and filled everywhere with glass-panels. People-flocks move together and apart and each person, whether together or apart, is probably the same person. I slide into Nordstrom and Aaron and Erik follow. I imagine people coming apart into many simple pieces. It's a stupid thought. There are lego-blocks in my mind. A woman says, "Welcome to Nordstrom's." I look at the perfume-counter and the glass perfume-bottles there in dozens of colors. Behind the perfume-bottles are two brunettes wearing very articulate make-up. I study them carefully and wonder what kind of make-up's very articulate make-up. The brunettes know I'm in the wrong store and soon they'll escort me outside to the parking-lot, slim fingers gripping my shoulders, one hand for each shoulder, fingers spread gently at my collar-bones, near my throat, perfect lips pursed in little ironic frowns. There's the sound everywhere of talking. A graying man plays a shiny Steinway and the man playing the Steinway's wearing a black tuxedo and tight white gloves. Or maybe his hands are only very white. I can't see. Aaron and Erik move slowly behind me and I'm moving very slowly and above us the long fluorescent-light-tubes are vibrating in a slow and cordial way. "The hands are just white," I say.

"What?" Erik asks.

"I don't know what I'm saying. Feel like doing something terrible."

Aaron looms over me and touches my shoulder then leans his face very nearby, breathing warmly on my neck. He might have one-million pores. Each pore might connect to other pores, beneath his skin, like a thousand twisting tunnels. "It's not possible to be terrible. No such thing as terrible," Aaron says.

"She's just moody." Erik's scratching the back of his hand, eyeing the brunettes. "Just wants attention. She's bored, bored and wants attention." I think of Erik naked. He said this of me once before. He stood quietly in the bathroom, naked, holding a hairbrush. "You just want attention," he said.

"I could kill you—you can't stop me from killing you," I say to Erik. "I could kill anyone and it'd be easy." I move behind a dress-rack and take my knife from my purse and slash the dresses. I start with a striped sundress. "I can kill these dresses if I want."

"Stop that," Aaron says. Aaron's head swivels, his eyes sweeping the store.

I continue to slash dresses. I search out flowers, sashes, ruffles. I search out gray and black, or pink. I undo pleats. Remove buttons. Sever straps.

"Just leave her alone," says Erik.

"I can't."

"She'll stop eventually. She's circumspect, I think. Does this all the time. Once we got kicked out of Hot Topic for the same shit. Told the manager the clothes looked sad."

A thick man moves nearby then angles away from us. "Merry Christmas," Aaron says respectfully.

I slash the dresses and cut tiny pieces from the dresses and put the dresses-pieces in my pockets. I thrust my knife through the dresses and rip the dresses. I squat on the floor and slash the carpet and stab the carpet and the carpet's very thick and full and brown and I pull up triangular carpet-flaps and cut them loose and put carpet-triangles into my pockets with the dresses-pieces.

"Let's go," Aaron says.

"No."

"I don't want to get caught."

Erik shrugs.

"Who cares if we get caught?" I say. I toss a dress onto the floor. "There, covered it."

Erik starts to laugh.

I put my knife away. Aaron and Erik are watching me so I watch Aaron and Erik and my eyes and their eyes are sort of motionless in the way that eyes can be motionless and still move suddenly. I open my mouth and breathe deeply and lean back and open my mouth further until I can't open my mouth any more and I push the air from my lungs violently and form the air into a sound and say the sound until my throat hurts and say the sound so that Aaron and Erik both are shocked and Erik shushes me and they hold their arms rigidly at their sides in a useless way and I pass them and push the air from my lungs and say the sound until I'm outside where it's cold and cloudy. Then I stop and laugh and wait for Aaron and Erik to find me. I want them to find me laughing. I touch the dresses-pieces in my pockets and the dresses-pieces are soft and warm. Aaron and Erik are moving toward me with their hands in their pockets and Aaron's ahead of Erik and very wide so that Erik almost disappears behind him. I touch my cell-phone and the dresses-pieces and the leather of my purse, the tiny triangles of carpet. I move these things together and let them touch each other.

SEVEN

Aaron's driving his Lexus, Erik next to him fiddling with the equalizer, the auto-tuner, shuffling CDs in the CD-changer— Sister Christian plays a while then It Was a Good Day. I'm lying in back, my head against the window. It's begun, slowly, to snow, and the cars around us move carefully along the highway. Drivers furrow brows and chew lips, and one man with a red moustache mouths something wordless with spittle then stares in a challenging way so I look down at my lap until he disappears. Aaron seems distant, somehow alien, robotic. In my mind he removes his head and trades it with another. He has a row of heads in a long hallway. There's a glass case, a thousand glass cases, an old man in a flag who removes the heads Aaron chooses. The old man is Aaron too. "How old's Aaron?" I ask.

"This's a nice-ass car," Erik says. "I'll have a car like this some day. How much was it? Thirty-thousand or something?"

"Do you feel old all the time?" I ask. "Does it hurt, now, when you wake? Do you roll out of bed, feeling sore and tired, groaning, you know, covered in sweat?" I consider these questions. "Do you think all the time or suddenly stop thinking? I'd stop thinking, I think. I'd worry I was going to die. I'd turn off."

"I don't know." Aaron's very intent on the road. His little clear eyes

33

are focused and hard and I want suddenly to poke Aaron's eyes, to test the hardness of Aaron's eyes, to rub Aaron's pupils with my fingertip.

"I love cars," Erik says. "I could make cars. I should be a car-designer. I could design this car. I'd change the color, add fins, lower the suspension maybe, new steering wheel, chrome, lots of chrome."

"I'll be old soon, but so what?" I say. "It probably doesn't matter."

"I put the rims on her car, tell Aaron how I put rims on your car, and the stereo, I did the stereo." Erik looks at me over his shoulder. "Tell him about the woofers. About the box." Erik touches the dashboard, the windshield, the seat. "I can design things. I have a good eye."

"I have life-insurance," Aaron says. "I have insurance for everything. Anything could happen. You could run over someone, get robbed, mugged, or home-invasion. I worry about home-invasion sometimes."

"Stuff," I say. "Stuff, stuff," I say.

"I used to make model cars sometimes, low-riders."

"Anyone could be a home-invader," Aaron says.

"I could be a home-invader." Home-invaders are bearded in dirty Levis and rollerblades.

"Crack-heads, you know, with your laptop or your TV."

"Leather interior low-riders."

"Sometimes I imagine fighting home-invaders, like I find them in the kitchen and sort of punch their faces, wrestle the guns away." Aaron's silent for a while. "Where're we going?"

"Don't know," Erik answers. "I don't know anything."

Erik's face seems suddenly very broad. I could trade faces with Erik. With Bill Murray. We could do it in a field in Montana. Aaron and

34

Erik are talking about home-invasion, about Unsolved Mysteries, how they'd break the arms of the home-invaders, take the guns or knives, tie the home-invaders to empty chaise-lounges, or place them carefully in the trunks of their cars, drive around town for a while, by the docks, or out to an abandoned field, near a barn, an old silo maybe, silver and bullet shaped, to place the home-invaders there, to lay them out in a bed of hay, tied down in chaise-lounges, and to use then their guns and knives. I don't have any guns but I could be a home-invader. I could wear roller-blades. Something to pull me then. A little Honda. I think about Mother instead. She wasn't a home-invader. I think about the rusty minivan, about backseats and Anastasia and Merna and the seatbelts and crisscrossing the seatbelts and the knees, exposed knees in the summer, bumping together, and the wind from the window-crack and the very warm very yellow sunlight through the window and the relaxing just-before with sleepy eyes and deep body-yawns in late afternoon. We drove through the Rockies to Montana when I was ten or twelve. Mother at the wheel, Father sleeping quietly in the front passenger-seat. Merna read to Anastasia from teen-magazines—manicures, dating, how to tease your bangs, how to be beautiful. I let my head flop to the side and sat very still and made my eyes flutter then close and stopped my breathing and waited for my sisters to shake me.

"Don't," Anastasia said.

"She's dead." Merna pushed me. "She's really dead now. People just die like that sometimes. The speed's too much for their brains." I didn't react, but remained very still, allowing Merna's pushes to move me slackly until I flopped over Anastasia's lap.

"See, she's dead," Merna said. "Anastasia, you killed her."

"Stop," Anastasia said.

Later we pulled into a gas-station and I hid behind the backseat, beneath our backpacks and tents and travel gear. I made myself still and quiet and relaxed and smelled the tent and sleeping bags, the cooler, the stuffed backpacks that smelled of mold and mildew and dirt. I wanted then to smell that way, to lie quietly in the unmoving wetness of those smells. This is probably what death smells like, I thought. Nobody'll ever find me here, I thought. I waited for Merna to uncover me, for Mother or Father to search me out, to remove carefully the sleeping bags, tents, backpacks, to stack them outside in the parking-lot, and to find me curled up and sleepy and cold. For Anastasia to say quietly, "Stop," and to cry then in Merna's lap. I could hug them, could sprawl my body over their bodies, could wait passively to be moved from one somewhere to another. The tents did not move. The sleeping bags remained still. I woke there later, beneath the tent, beneath the sleeping bags, the backpacks. I was cold and wet, hearing only the rough vibration of the van over concrete.

EIGHT

"Stop here," I say. It's an AM/PM.

"Don't need gas," Aaron says.

"Stop here," I say. "I don't want to pee all over your leather seats. It's probably disrespectful or something."

"I could get a soda," Erik says. "I could get some Twinkies."

Inside the AM/PM there are many rows with neatly stacked Snickers and Reese's Pieces, then aspirin and ibuprofen, and along the wall a rack of magazines. A boy's leafing through a copy of Guns & Ammo. I can see the uncovered tops of Penthouse and Barely Legal. Near the cash-register, hotdogs and sausages slowly turn beneath a heat-lamp on long metal rollers. The cashier's very young with a shaved head and a very narrow chin. He stares at me and I stare back, and at the same time I'm conscious of Aaron and Erik behind me. Aaron's holding the door and Erik's moving toward the Twinkies, his fingers twitching in typing motions.

"Where's your restroom?" I ask

"Over there." The cashier wiggles his wet brown eyes toward a little dark hallway off the corner of the store, next to the beer-cooler.

I move into the restroom and lock the door. Tiny hairs line the sink, spread out at the edges then gather together in blotches near the drain.

The mirror's scratched. One scratch says, 'I love tampons,' and another says, 'Eat monkeys bitch.' I sit on the toilet in a peculiar way, holding my body inches above the seat. I consider home-invasion. I think for a while of monkeys and tampons. When I'm done, I scratch a message into the mirror with my knife. I scratch, 'Birthday-invasion.' This makes me feel energetic, like I'll have to walk sideways through doors, like I'll walk very straight through narrow hallways, smash white-haired men into concrete walls, overturn their oxygen-tanks, their little silver walkers, ignoring the grunts of pain and angry glares, just walk very straight until, finally, I must stop. I'm in the narrow hallway. Erik's at the register with money. Aaron's reading People near the door, Bill Murray seeming to stare out from his chest. I watch the back of the cashier's head and move along the aisles, my hands carefully placing Snickers, Kit-Kats, Tylenol, anything, into my waistband, pockets, then in my armpits and everywhere I can think. When I move, I make small crackling noises but I ignore them. I move behind Erik, and breathe on Erik's neck. Erik's still paying and the cashier's staring at the counter.

"Have you ever been robbed?" I ask. Aaron starts to frown and I glare at him. "Have you ever been robbed with a knife? I bet people come in with knives all the time, point them at you and say something like, 'I'm taking the Twinkies. Close your eyes or I'll stab your face.' That's what I'd say, I think, if I wanted free Twinkies. I mean look at Erik, ready to pay for his Twinkies, but he could just pull out a knife and suddenly stab your face, throw gasoline on you, light it with a lighter, you know, like that lighter on the counter."

Erik looks at me sideways and says, "My name's fucking Todd."

"No," the cashier says.

"No what?"

"Never been robbed or anything. People are nice here. It's like Nice-land."

I push Erik away from me. "Hands up bitch, this is a robbery." I pull out my switch-blade.

Aaron's laughing. He grabs my arm and says, "Let's go."

"She's kidding," Erik says. "Don't worry, we'll take her home. She's drunk. Whole bottle of vodka, fifteen minutes. She's small, but an amazing drinker."

"I'm going to stab his face. Punk-bitch."

"We're sorry," Erik says.

"Don't call the police," Aaron says. "Please?"

They drag me from the store. I wave my switch-blade. I want to scare the cashier. I want him to be full of fear, in pain with fear, to wonder whenever a girl walks into the AM/PM if this is the day he'll be stabbed in the face, to warn the other cashiers about small quiet girls with switch-blades who want to burn them with gasoline. As Aaron drives out of the parking-lot and merges onto the highway, I pull the Snickers, Kit-Kats, and Tylenol from my waistband. I find other things, lighters, tree-shaped air-fresheners, Pepsi. "I got all this stuff in my clothes," I say. "Want some stuff? It's good stuff." I open a Snickers. "Why'd you stop me? I had a plan."

"Don't be ridiculous," Aaron says.

"Just stop it." Erik stares blankly out the window and sighs, then drags his fingers along the window. "Shit," he says to Aaron. "Motherfucker."

"I'm not crazy. I only wanted to scare him a little." I slide down onto the floor. "I'm hiding," I say. "You can't see me." Outside the window the Douglas-firs are tall and shadowy. I could climb the trees with special spiked climbing-boots, live there, train pigeons to bring food and water. Steal pigeon-eggs from nearby nests, make my own person-nest and live warm and alone. "Don't you want to say something ever, sometimes?" I say. "It's my birthday and I wanted to say something beautiful and paralyzing to the little cashier so he'd remember me and think of me sometimes, alone at night, or with his girlfriend, and feel this great paralyzing fear and later dream of little girls with switch-blade-knives and gasoline. Now he's just a bored little boy behind a cash-register forever."

Aaron eyes the road. Snow-flakes drift there and swirl before his headlights. "Stealing's stupid," Aaron says. "Increases retail pricing. Seriously, this is a business fact. You're only giving some corporation more reasons to take money from everyone, from poor people mostly. If you were a man, you wouldn't get away with that shit."

"Oh yeah?"

"Shit. Probably people are always nice to you cause of your tits."

Erik doesn't say anything. Erik's eyes are closed and his breathing's very even.

"You don't know anything," I say.

"I know no one can take you seriously. I don't believe anything you say. Don't even know your name. You'd lie anyway."

"I thought we had a deal. I thought you were taking me to Lisbon."

Aaron doesn't answer. It's late afternoon. Traffic has become thicker and the cars moves slowly, heavily forward, like little robot-glaciers. Snow has gathered in dirty piles along the edges of the road, edged then with clear wet slush. There's a hissing as the cars roll through the wetness. I wonder what it would be like to lie in the slush, to let it soak slowly through my sweater, to look down at my hand beneath the slush and to see it there, framed somehow, pale and cold.

"Take the next right," I say.

"Why."

"Please. You'd just think I'm lying anyway." Aaron turns right. The road curves gently and slopes down among large gray houses and thick brown trees. "Turn right again," I say. "There." Aaron turns again. The road curves gently and slopes down among large gray houses and thick brown trees. Each house looks like the same house with little green snow-speckled lawns and large two-car garages and red-brick facades. The road continues to curve and slope in precisely the same way as before, with the same angles and grades. Some houses have lights and people, inside and outside, and some houses are dark and empty. I hum through my nose and move around in my seat. "There," I say to Aaron. "Right there."

Aaron glances at me, then at Erik. Erik's sleeping noisily against the window. Aaron says, "I'm sorry about what I said. I shouldn't have said what I said."

I make a complacent face.

"Where are we going?"

I watch Aaron's large red nose and imagine removing the nose somehow, placing the nose in a little golf-ball display-case, placing it center-perfect on a brick-mantle.

"Home-invasion," I say.

NINE

The house sits at the base of two hills surrounded by identical two-story houses, separated only by tall chain-link fences. There are two separate attics, hundreds of segmented windows, a two-car garage. A neat hexagonal lawn before it, lined with brown shrubs, dead snow-covered flowers, a narrow pumice-border. I tell Aaron to stop. "We're here," I say. But I feel desperate and disappointed and I think the word, home-invasion. My body's not tensed or vibrating and I'm not anything so I hold my hands in a little knot and carefully stop my thoughts.

Erik snores against the window.

"Where are we?" Aaron asks.

"Here," I say again. "We're here, here," I say.

The garage-doors are open. I study the matching silver Cadillacs. From hooks in the garage-ceiling hang two bicycles—curved handlebars, black brake-lines, toothy pedals. Along the garage-walls are steel grids from which hang power-drills, hammers, screwdrivers, skill-saws, routers, spare blades—packaged and unpackaged—then drill-bits, bolt-cutters, a rake—all blue or gray or a dull silver and marred here and there with dirt or oil. There are no flags. I open the car-door and slowly step onto the icy sidewalk, then move toward the garage. There are no icy garages in Lisbon. Parking-lots and driveways are theoretically the same thing. Could one transport you to the other? A line of light slants beneath the door that leads from the garage into the house, an elongated light-rectangle very thin and asymmetrical. I move toward it.

"Wait," says Aaron.

"Yeah wait," Erik says. Erik's awake and standing. His face is very tight and small and wrinkled, slack somehow, like folded bed-sheets sliding slowly from a closet shelf. "Where the fuck are we?"

I move forward. I can feel Aaron and Erik's bodies approaching, but when I turn Aaron and Erik's bodies are still distant so I continue into the garage. Over my shoulder, Aaron and Erik's faces are little red balls floating above their necks. The mouths on the little red balls open and close rhythmically. I can't hear any words. Their mouths move secretly and I want suddenly to be the mouths, to understand mouth-movements, to form solid, specific words with the mouths and later to write the words in my diary. My hand's on the doorknob, my thumb pressing the keyed lock. I could write 'Lisbon doorknob' somewhere. I could write 'flag safety.' Anastasia once told me it was good luck to touch all doorknobs—that if you miss a doorknob you'd probably die. I didn't believe her and tried for many years to touch no doorknobs. "That's stupid," I said. I was small and my hair was long and thickly braided.

"It's true," Anastasia said. "Everything's true."

I followed Anastasia into the backyard and onto the rough patio where we sat cross-legged, knee to knee and watched worker-ants in the brown grass-patches. We wore white crepe skirts that fluttered when we moved and the sky was a soft blanket above us, wide and long so that no matter where we looked there was the sky falling down.

"Don't be so gullible," I said. "I could say, 'You're the ant-queen' and that wouldn't make you an ant-queen."

"I'd be kind of an ant-queen."

"Really? How?"

"If you tell me something then the thing you told me is a real thing and real things are always true."

I looked dumbly at Anastasia. "Follow me," I said. I walked slowly into the garage, this garage, and Anastasia followed. We moved crab-like between the Cadillacs. I leaned against a bare white wall-sliver and removed a battery-operated power-drill from the wall-grid, then held it there in my hand. "You're a robot," I said. "We put you together on your birthday. You came in a kit from Wal-Mart because I wanted a new sister. There was this ad—you were so pretty in the ad." Anastasia didn't answer. She leaned against our mother's Cadillac. I imagined opening its four heavy doors, sprawling Anastasia lengthwise across the massive windshield, strapping her down with pink bungee-cords. "I made your head. That was my job. I used this power-drill to make your head." I showed her the drill, pulled the trigger for a moment, listened to the whirring buzz of it. "There were complicated instructions and I couldn't read well so I probably made some mistakes, which is why you're broken probably. I don't think it's fixable, not completely, but that's okay. I know I should love all moving things. And really I love you. Your little head." I adjusted the drill-bit in the chuck and tightened it. "Anyway, I'm bored now and I'm going to take this head apart. It's okay. Don't move even a little. I'll fix everything." I pulled the trigger and stepped forward.

"Don't worry about the pain. Shouldn't hurt that much, and anyway you're a robot and so can't really feel pain. Pain, for you, is just part of your programming and nothing much to worry about. I know these things."

"Don't," Anastasia said. "Please."

But I did.

First, I removed the eyes.

Set carefully on a nearby shelf, Anastasia's eyes were very large and round—like billiard-balls, maybe—and the eyes were soft and pliable and I pushed them with my fingers and my fingers pushed into Anastasia's eyes, through the irises, the pupils, and Anastasia's eyes began to leak slowly a clear fluid, as though punctured. The eyes shrank and became shriveled things, prune or raisin-like. They dried there on the shelf, staining the wood. I touched them and touched them again. I kept them in pockets, wrapped them in a white silk scarf. I took them to school, showed them to the other girls beneath my flip-up desk-top. Placed them in a shoe-box diorama, surrounded on all sides by tiny mirrors, shined on them a little LED flashlight. The mirrors, the light, all within the shoebox together with the little shriveled eyes.

Erik's touching my shoulder softly from the side and Aaron's staring directly into my eyes.

"You stopped," Aaron says.

"You said something," Erik says. "But I couldn't hear what you said."

"Nothing," I say. "I was thinking something." I touch the door. "Home-invasion?"

"Why this house?" Aaron asks.

"Because they're rich. The house's huge. They're rich and have things we can take—laptops probably, televisions, gold watches, platinum mirrors. We'll go to the pawnshop and get rich."

"Who lives here?"

"They live here. Them."

Aaron watches me. "Why're we here?" His voice is monotone.

"I removed Anastasia's eyes with a power-drill," I say. "Maybe I was thirteen then or something, maybe fourteen. I put them here once, on a shelf." I open the door into the house. There's a long hallway with hardwood floors and a high white ceiling and very flat white walls, all well-lighted with regularly placed fixtures made to look like torches but instead of fire there are fluorescent light-bulbs. "Follow me," I say. I step into the hallway. I listen to my shoes on the hardwood floor.

TEN

I lived alone in the house for a year. I was fifteen. Merna was at college. Anastasia dead. My parents were vacationing in the Virgin Islands or something and my grandparents were to be my caretakers. I came home from school and found my grandparents cold and unmoving in the family-room, naked, sprawled on the sofa, their vein-y, wrinkled legs tangled together. I called Mother and told her. Mother laughed. "You're so funny..." I called Merna. Merna said, "Don't call me again, bitch." I laid the bodies on the carpet, crossed their arms over their chests, and closed their eyes. I placed an old white sheet over them, head to toe, so I could see only their tented human forms. Turned off the lights, switched off electricity at the breaker. After I carried the TV into the kitchen, I closed all the family-room doors and carefully placed thick bath-towels beneath the doors and removed the door-knobs, then filled the doors' knob-less holes with cardboard and old torn-up t-shirts. There were cans of white paint in the garage. I took them and painted the family-room doors so they appeared solid, wall-like. I called my parents and told them what I'd done. "Don't lie," Mother said. "If you lie like that someday you'll turn into a dirty rotten slut." Mother paused. "All dirty sluts are liars and all liars are dirty sluts."

"No Mom," I said. "I did it, really."

"Don't call me again, okay?" Mother said. "We don't have time for this shit, this kind of slut-shit. Why don't you do something useful? Okay?"

I walked two miles along a winding, tree-lined hill to Safeway. I wore loose jeans and a rain-parka and I filled my rain-parka with apples and oranges, mushrooms, tofu, carrots. It was better to steal healthy food. I chewed my food slowly. I got almonds. I got little bottles of Naked orange-juice. I drank tall glasses of water. Before Trigonometry I said to my teacher, "I'm quitting. You won't see me here anymore, at school."

"Not really allowed to quit, you know. There are laws. Besides, next week is vectors." He looked at my hands very carefully. "Vectors!" he said.

"I'm moving to Tibet. My parents are Buddhists and we're going to learn meditation from this really famous monk in Tibet for a year and become better, more centered people. Vegan Tibetan monks. We'll raise sheep. I think I am supposed to learn 'enlightenment.' Also, how to make sweaters. I'm not sure how it works, but I think the sheep help."

"Oh."

I nodded. "Enlightenment's pretty difficult."

My teacher's eyes became very active and his hands clenched into fists repeatedly until he stepped to the whiteboard and began erasing equations in an orderly way. He erased variables alphabetically, then numbers from least to greatest. "Vectors are really dynamite. You could really learn a lot. Trajectories, you know. People swimming against a current..." On his desk was a silver ball-point pen with a very sharp tip. I placed the pen in my pocket and held it there. I stayed home whenever possible. With the pen, I made shopping-lists. The lists were alphabetical and always started with almonds. Late Saturday nights, I took the shopping-lists to Safeway. On Sundays I called Merna. "Today I stole apples and pears and carrots and lettuce and a pineapple and a cantaloupe. And almonds, bags of fucking almonds. Hundreds of them."

"I told you not to call me," Merna would say.

"I've become enlightened. Meditate three times a day. I don't eat, and can levitate now. Sometimes, anyway. I have this herd of sheep in the backyard."

"Good for you, bitch-face."

In the garage, I built a dollhouse, three feet high, five feet wide, a detailed miniature version of this house with tall, segmented windows and hardwood floors, plush gray carpeting, the two-car garage, the two peaked attics. I made little boys and girls, tiny leather loveseats, soft brown beds, triangular flags, and arranged everything as it should be within the dollhouse. I called Mother and told her about the dollhouse, the winding staircase, the miniature racing bicycles. "It's perfect," I said. "It has everything."

"You're such a lying slut."

I kept the dollhouse in the backyard, mounted on a low brick pedestal. I lined the roof with real shingles, sealed the wood to protect it from rain and snow. Each night I sat cross-legged before the dollhouse, meditating. I raised little pink flags over the dollhouse. I sewed new flags, almond themed, almond-vectors, hung them from the bedroom walls. Sometimes I would reach in and make small corrections, refold a sheet, move the television. Repaint and reseal the doors that led into the family-room.

49

Merna was to return from college soon for the summer. I soaked the dollhouse with gasoline. Trailed lighter-fluid from the dollhouse and sat calmly, cross-legged in the grass and lighted it with my zippo-lighter, then watched the dollhouse burn into tiny ashes. "Beautiful," I said then, as the ashes floated, vector-like, in air-currents. "Beautiful," I say now.

"What?" Aaron says.

I tell him about my grandparents and the dollhouse. I say something about almonds.

He's shaking his head.

I watch the shaking head.

ELEVEN

Beyond the hallway is the foyer. To the right is the carpeted family-room, separated by a low wooden railing, sunk into the floor, three steps down. To the left is the main entrance, a wide oak door with a four-panel stained-glass window depicting the flight of doves over a shallow pond. Hanging from the ceiling above the entrance is a silver chandelier with hundreds of tiny light-bulbs.

I jump into the family-room. I jump onto the piano.

"Get off." Aaron looks wildly around and then angles his head as though listening for sound or movement.

"Let's destroy the piano," I say. "Help me push it outside. I have lighter-fluid. There's gasoline in the garage. We can burn the whole thing on the patio. Take the furniture to the patio and burn the furniture with lighter-fluid and make a big pile of burnt furniture and pianos and stuff. You know, a bonfire." I hop to the floor and push the piano. The piano doesn't move.

"Come on," Erik says. "Quit it."

"Whoever these people are, are probably home," Aaron says. "I don't know where they are but they're here, and if they come in here, what're we going to do? Kill everyone? Tie them to chairs, torture them or something? Too dangerous. Let's go to a movie. This's stupid anyway. I've

51

let it go too far." Aaron falls heavily onto the wide sofa. His torso falls at a different speed than his arms, his head, and each part of Aaron's falling at different speeds. The sofa slides a little and hits the wall. Aaron's narrow, fatless head flops over the sofa-top and his wide fat body sinks into the sofa until the sofa springs back and holds Aaron's body in place. "This is nice," Aaron says. "I don't want to burn this."

"My grandparents died on that sofa."

Aaron holds the sofa-arm, pulls the sofa-arm fabric, moves the fabric side to side, rubs the fabric. "Nice sofa."

"Erik," I say. "Make love to me on the piano."

"What?"

"It'll be entertaining, for Aaron."

Erik looks confused and moves away from me. "I can't," Erik says. Erik moves into the hallway, leans against the wall, hands thrust in pockets. "My name's Todd."

I sit at the piano and push the piano-keys and listen to the piano-key sounds which are high-pitched and raw. I push piano-keys in a rhythmic way but with no regard for sound or beauty. "This is my step-parents' house," I say. "They're probably sleeping. My step-parents sleep all day. They're very boring. And they can't move from their bed because their bed's so comfortable and it's painful for them to move and especially to see people or watch television. They're hiding from us. My step-parents hide from everybody. They're terrified that murderers will come, masked maybe, with nylons, and burn them in their bed or even tie them to the bed and cut small pieces from their little faces until they slowly, painfully bleed to death, and especially they're terrified of bleeding in the bed and staining their very soft satin sheets. I told them about bloodstains I made on satin sheets once and how hard they were to clean and they're terrified for their bed which is very expensive, an import from Lisbon." Aaron and Erik aren't listening. Erik has moved to the sofa and is sitting next to Aaron. Aaron holds the remote-control. On the television, a women with fine wrinkles and plump red lips cries into her hands. Her blouse is blindingly white. Behind the women, a young man with wide white teeth and symmetrical facial features paces with his hands in his pockets. The symmetrical young man shakes his head and says, "It had to be done. I had to do it. Me." I don't know anything. People who are symmetrical are happier than people who aren't symmetrical. "I'm asymmetrical and it's really really terrible," I say.

Erik looks at me, then back at the television.

"Scary symmetry," I say. I think about that.

Aaron says, "Sshhh."

"Steal everything," I say. There's a sound. On the stairs, I see a foot. My stepmother's foot. When I was very young, she beat me with a ball peen hammer. She took me to the garage. "Stand there," she would say. She would get the hammer. "Bend over," she would say. I would bend over between the Cadillacs. "This might hurt," she would say. "Hold your goddamn ankles." I would hold my ankles. I would stare fixedly in the Cadillac's mirror and watch her red mottled face over my shoulder. "Something, somewhere..." I say.

"Sshhh," Erik says.

I can see the ankle on the stairs and the knee, then the hem of the thick terrycloth-bathrobe. The waist with its tie and slowly the bulge of

53

breasts, shoulders. The little wrinkled head above the bathrobe. Long gray hair pulled into a tight pony-tail and draped carefully over one shoulder. My stepmother can see me with her little gray eyes and it's terrifying and I'm terribly aware of her terrible wrinkles. "You came," she says with a little delighted smile. "I didn't think you'd come, you never come by anymore. I'm so happy you came."

"I came."

"Who's this? Who're these people?"

"It's Aaron and Erik. They're my lovers."

"You're terrible," she says. She steps down into the family-room and holds out her finely wrinkled hand to Aaron and Aaron takes her hand and their hands are shaking. "I'm Stella," she says. She looks at Aaron and Erik and Aaron and Erik watch her in a curious way. The television's bright and lighted behind them. On the television, the beautiful, finely-wrinkled woman's crying into her old and useless hands. My stepmother smiles at me. She says, "I'm the old, useless grandmother."

TWELVE

"You are not."

I've said the words but Aaron and Erik aren't listening. Together with Stepmother, Aaron and Erik watch a little girl shakedown three mafia gangsters for Pepsi-cola on television. If Merna were here, she might corroborate each person's identity. Maybe everybody's somebody else. Maybe nobody told me. "You're my stepmother," I say.

She sighs. "Maybe I am. But I'm really also your grandmother."

"If you're my grandmother then where's Grandfather?"

"Sshhh," Erik says. "I'm watching commercials."

"I just want to know something."

"Sshhh," they say. Their eyes are fixed on the television. Tide, now available in a condensed formula. We can save the earth with smaller bottles. This is very reasonable. Everything could be smaller. There's a beach and it's bright and clean, waves breaking over a black rock. The beach could be smaller, with triangular flags. New Mexico. I step into the kitchen. Here the hardwood flooring continues, broken only by a wide island with a built-in double-sink. The countertops are black marble. The refrigerator and the double-oven are a dull, lightless metal, stainless-steel I think, and perfectly clean. The cabinet-doors have partitioned glass windows through which I see rows of white plates, saucers, and serving-dishes stacked neatly in specially designed holders. I stand quietly in front of the refrigerator. From the refrigerator-door I take mayonnaise, ranch-dressing, mustard, soy-sauce, rice-wine, and nacho-cheese, then a tiny bottle of tiny pickles, and arrange them on the countertop in a row, from shortest to tallest. I remove lettuce, tomatoes, and one banana and stack these on the row of condiments. I get more from the refrigerator. I get milk, orange-juice, tofu. I get yogurt and marmalade. I get baking-soda. I move and arrange them, construct a miniature countertop-castle, then observe and consider the castle. I want suddenly to display the castle for Stepmother and Grandfather, to photograph the castle, me standing quietly before it, expressionless. Then with Aaron and Erik, then Stepmother, Grandfather, Merna. Arms crossed, mouths in tight little lines. To publish the castle-photos in the New York Times, to take the New York Times somewhere, New Mexico maybe, and show it to homeless boys. To slowly strangle these homeless boys in an alleyway maybe, or teach them to read. To make gifts of the boys to childless Wal-Mart store-managers. The children wrapped carefully in plain white sheets. Is there a ribbon? I sweep the castle violently to the floor. There's a noise and a mess.

"What the hell's going on in there?" Stepmother says.

"Nothing."

She comes into the kitchen. Aaron follows Erik. The kitchen's warm and hurried and the air's more precious here as each person breathes their share away.

"I'm sorry. I'll clean it up."

"Don't worry about it," Stepmother says. "Somebody'll take care of it later." Aaron pushes the lettuce around with his foot. "Let me show you boys something," Stepmother says. "Meet me in the family-room in five minutes. I have this thing I'm going to show you." She walks away.

I follow Aaron and Erik into the family-room. "Don't listen to anything she says. She's crazy. She married into the family for the money or something, but she's crazy. Lived in this psych-ward place after a psychotic-break." I watch as they sit on the sofa. I pace before them. "She stole her roommate's Toyota, in college, right out of the dorm parking-lot, then crashed into her roommate. This young, thin girl named Darla whose spine was crushed. Paraplegic, now, because of her. We used to visit her sometimes at the convalescent home. Take her on walks in the park, in her wheelchair. All because she failed her Communications exam and tried to mutilate her own face with a knife. Killed a dozen chickens, ate them raw."

"This is a really nice television," Erik says. "Flat-screen. I want to get a flat-screen sometime. I wonder if it's LCD or plasma."

"Are they different?" Aaron says. He's sitting. Aaron examines the sofa with his hands. "This fabric's really soft, first-rate. I have one like this, different color, sort of dark-brown. Something about sofas, you know."

"LCD means liquid-crystal-display," Erik says. He walks over to the television, touches the screen. "I used to have this digital-watch with liquid-crystal-display. Really amazing the way humans make things with crystals."

"I'm serious. Don't listen to her. She's crazy. We could steal everything, that TV, the sofa, and sell it at a pawnshop, make money, go someplace else. New Mexico maybe, Lisbon. Help me tie her up when she comes back. We'll tie her up in the kitchen, to a chair."

"I wonder where they got the sofa. I wonder if it's the same place I got mine. Maybe they got a special deal? Do you know? I always feel like I'm missing out on the special deals. Like I always have to pay full price. I could have more money if I had time to watch for sales, if I kept coupons."

"Gag and blind her, leave her starving alone."

"They don't have furniture coupons, though. Do they?" Aaron begins to remove cushions, to search the sofa-cracks with his hands. "So nice," he says. Aaron's arms are very long and active and Aaron's head's moving side to side quickly and the cushions are scattered on the floor behind him. "Soft," Aaron says. "Isn't there a label somewhere? It's illegal to remove labels, you know. There's got to be a label here somewhere."

Erik looks carefully at my face. "This is a really really nice house. I'll have a house like this some day. How come you never took me here? I always wanted to meet your grandparents. Ashamed of me or something? I'm probably not good enough. Maybe if I were going to college or something. If I made like twenty dollars an hour or something, right? Didn't you like the stereo I put in your car? You didn't, did you?"

"I don't know what you mean."

"Something," Erik says. He shoves the cushions aside with his foot.

I can hear Stepmother's feet padding on the hardwood floor. She's wearing a white flower-print jumper now and her arms are holding a large brown scrapbook. "Darla," I say. "You're going to show the dead-Darla pictures to my little lovers?" I move to Stepmother and reach for the scrapbook. "She took Polaroids of Darla after she ran her down. It's disgusting. Stop and give it. No dead-Darla pictures. No dead-Darla."

"What are you talking about?"

Aaron has fixed the sofa and Aaron and Erik are sitting on the sofa, their hands folded on their laps. Stepmother steps down into the family-room, cradling the scrapbook.

"This is a really nice sofa," Aaron says.

"Thank you."

"Stop," I say. "Just stop everything."

Stepmother sits between Aaron and Erik and opens the scrapbook. They all lean forward. I walk upstairs, watching them until the angles are wrong. There's a hallway with seven white doors. I open my bedroom door. In the far corner there's a narrow bed with gray sheets and a dark blue patchwork quilt next to a dark three-drawer nightstand. I keep a knife in the nightstand, in the back corner of the top drawer behind my panties, taped there beneath a knife-sized strip of cardboard. I was ten when I stole the knife. I slept over at Mallory's. Her hair was dark and curly and brown and she once said to me, "How come your hair isn't curly or brown and pretty like my hair is?" and I came to love her. I imagined stabbing her with the knife, then baseball-batting her head. I imagined tying a noose and hanging Sparkles, her little gray kitten, from her low porch. I knew I loved her then. I watched her in class and sat next to her on the playground at recess, touched her brown and curly hair with my little imperfect hands. It's a bread-knife with a round black handle and a long serrated blade. I found it in Mallory's kitchen, in a drawer that had many knives and many slots for other knives. There were too many knives. Even bread-knives the same size and shape as my knife. And my knife was clean and unused. Scratch-less, the handle smooth and new. It felt terrible that the knife was unused and I took it and hid it in my jean-jacket.

It's not always evil to kill things, I think.

I lie on my bed and look at the little plastic stars glued to my ceiling.

"Stars are evil," I say aloud.

THIRTEEN

There's a knock and Grandfather steps into the room. Grandfather's very tall and gaunt, his shoulders stooped. His red flannel shirt's baggy and tucked into his jeans which are loose and held up by a leather-belt on its final notch. "You're here," he says slowly. Grandfather moves to the chair and falls into it with a little sigh, his arms snaking over the chair-arms and resting there, the hands shaking on the edge of it. Grandfather's head's hairless and even his eyebrows seem sparse, barren somehow. His face becomes a round thing with parallel wrinkles. His mouth's a big black hole. "I'm going to die," he says.

"You always say that," I say, but I don't know if that's true. I try to remember Grandfather saying those same words before.

"The doctor says I'm dying. I have cancer. Says I'm like a 'cancer-garden' but that's okay. I've probably always had cancer. She uses me to teach new doctors at the hospital. I'm ready for it. My friends are pretty much all dead. My tree died, you know. The maple my father planted. Rotted through the middle. Had to have it chopped down before it fell on the house. House's old and dying too. Every week it's a new repair-man. New insulation. Replace the refrigerator. The drywall. Dry-rot. Only thing living well's the insects, because insects eat dead things I suppose. There're probably insects inside me eating my insides like I'm already dead. Like preparation or something. I don't know. Maybe god knows about death and stuff. The doctor kind of knows. I eat twenty different pills a day. The pills are probably made from dead animals, or animal-fat anyway. My brother died, you know. My last brother. He didn't have any kids or anything, so I'm the only one. And I go to the pharmacy once a week and I go to the doctor once a week. It's all scheduled very well."

"I'm dying too. I haven't told anyone yet."

"Don't be ridiculous. You're too young to be dying."

"Life's a long dying probably. I just thought that in my head and then said it and it sounds true. I probably read it somewhere."

"That's stupid." Grandfather begins to cough. "Teenagers... Just do something or other. Go somewhere and be a person. Steal a goddamn Cadillac."

"I'm not a teenager."

"Do you remember your sixteenth birthday party?"

I try to remember. I think the words, birthday caterpillar-sandwich. I think other words. "No, I don't think I ever had a party."

"We drove to Vancouver B.C., stayed in a hotel? Invited your high-school friend. Mallory? Went to the aquarium there. The beluga whales, that upside-down dolphin?"

"I don't remember."

"Doesn't matter anyway." Grandfather's hand reaches toward me. "Here," he says, "help me up." I grab Grandfather's hand and arm and pull him to his feet, and his hand and arm are very cold even through the flannel, and his flesh's soft and malleable. He groans as he stands, and he seems very lightweight and frail and I think I could easily lift him and carry him on my back. When I was very young Grandfather carried me around and tossed me into the air. Sometimes he caught me. Sometimes he let me fall. "You have to learn that people sometimes drop people and it hurts like fuck." Grandfather had black hair then, combed into a delicate pompadour and his face was lined and rigid like a metal grating. He shuffles out of the room. "Come downstairs," he says. Grandfather's hunched and can't see me. "We'll have coffee."

"In a minute. I'll be down in a minute."

I open my nightstand-drawer and loosen the cardboard, remove the bread-knife. I hold the bread-knife in my hand. It seems pale and flimsy now, a dollar-store bread-knife with little dents and nicks. I put the knife in my purse. I think about my sixteenth birthday in Canada. Mallory was there and beautiful in a white tank-top and red miniskirt, her bouncy curly hair cut into a bob. We stayed at the Westin, on the seventeenth floor. We shared a room and outside our window was a courtyard with a tall fountain. Five stone fish spit water into a shallow pool. I sat next to the window. Mallory lay on the bed. "This is Canada," I said. "I don't feel different."

"It's ugly here," Mallory said. "But it's ugly everywhere, so don't blame the Canadians."

"Do you think we can have wine with dinner?"

"It's your grandfather."

We drank wine with dinner and Mallory and I stumbled outside near the fountain with our arms laced together. There were bright white lights beneath the pooled water and the fish were wet and gleaming and spitting water-streams and we sat next to the fountain and leaned against each other, our hands holding other hands.

"You know what?" Mallory said.

"This fountain is a fountain, fountain," I said, laughing. "Fountain, fountain," I said again.

"I fucked the math-teacher in his classroom."

"Oh?"

"On his desk."

"Really?"

Mallory didn't answer. She stepped into the fountain. "There's money down here," she said. She dove under the water and grabbed all the quarters she could grab and put the quarters down the front of her tank-top. "Help me get the money," Mallory said.

"Stop. People are watching us."

"So fucking what?"

"I don't want people looking at me."

Mallory shook her head and dove under the water again, her hands feeling along the fountain-bottom for change and scooping it into her tank-top.

I went back to our hotel-room and sat by the window. Mallory was tiny and quiet as she dove into the water and grabbed quarters and nickels, then surfaced and chuckled at her good fortune. I wondered if anybody was watching Mallory. If anybody was watching me as I watched Mallory or if anybody was watching anybody with video-cameras or satellite-cameras or even with human-eyes. I was watching Mallory so somebody was watching Mallory and Mallory was watching only the scattered change at the fountain-bottom. I considered this and leaned my head against the window and half-closed my eyes so that everything but Mallory was a little gray blur. Then, Mallory slipped and fell forward, hit her head on the concrete fountain-edge. Little red drips fanned out along the concrete and Mallory slid slowly, drunkenly into the fountain-water. She lay there face down. Her little head and beautiful curly hair bobbed in the fountain-water and the fountain-water turned dark with little red bubbles.

FOURTEEN

"This is from the elementary school spring pageant. See: Cleopatra," Stepmother says. I'm on the stairs, against the wall. I can't see Aaron, Erik, Stepmother, or Grandfather, but I hear Grandfather cough hoarsely and apologize. I hear the slow turning of pages and the sound of old fingers and crinkling plastic. At my feet, a heating-vent forces warm air onto my ankles and up my skirt in a pleasant way and I crouch and lean back to maximize the warm airflow, holding my skirt around me to keep the warm air in. Stepmother's speaking again. "This is the home-coming dance when she was fifteen. The dress's so pretty. We made it together, kind of, and sewed it and designed it, and her little date is so handsome in his little tuxedo, don't you think?" Stepmother sighs a little sigh. "Look at this."

"Do you have photos of her parents?" Aaron asks.

There's a pause.

"Well..."

I run downstairs, jumping the last three and landing with a solid thump. "I'm back," I say. "What's everyone doing? Let's play Monopoly, or watch TV, sit together on the couch or something." Stepmother and Grandfather sit across from Aaron and Erik, the coffee table between them. "This is so family-like, like we're a family, just Stepmother, Grandfather, lover-Erik and lover-Aaron. We should take pictures for the scrapbook so we can have real memories and stuff." I squish between Aaron and Erik and feel Aaron and Erik's bodies against my body. We generate body-warmth and pass it through each other in a circuit.

"I'm your grandmother, not your stepmother."

"My name's Todd."

I don't answer. I turn on the television with the remote-control. "We should watch The Wire," I say. "One where the cops beat drug-dealers in the interrogation-room. I like interrogation-rooms." I think about interrogation-rooms. There are wide tables and steel chairs and bright, hot lights, or bright bare bulbs hanging from black cords, hundreds of them, so you have to crouch beneath them. There are wide windows with one-way glass, observers behind with notepads and cameras. Grandfather there, wearing a gray suit, his notepad clutched to his chest. Aaron's sitting at the table, leaning lazily in his chair, flopping his thin hair side to side, scratching slowly his forehead with a .45. Erik pacing in front of the one-way window, staring at his hands, his tongue at the corner of his mouth. I sit in the far chair clutching a bottle of water. "You don't fucking know what you're talking about," I would say. "I'm not even a real person." There's nothing on TV so I tell them about the interrogation-room but they ignore me so I sit cross-legged on the floor and watch as the pages of the scrapbook slowly flip. The pictures there are bright and orderly, chronological, and I can see my hair, brown and tight, or curled, then the dresses and jeans, and I see Merna next to me, often in sunlight, or lightless, in the yard, at parks, huddled together atop porches or hills, in the back of a minivan somewhere I don't recognize. Grandmother there, but Grandfather always absent because he's the eye. I think he's the eye.

FIFTEEN

"You're not even a real person," I said. Father and I were on Alcatraz Island. It was summer vacation. "You're an android or something. Designed by government-androids to make me think I'm human. We're in a lab and I'm the variable aren't I?" I stepped into a cell and closed the iron-gate. Pulled my face against the cold bars. "Take a picture of me in the cell," I said. "If you can handle it, not being human and all?"

"Sshhh," Father said. "I'm listening to the audio-tour." He adjusted his headphones.

"I am the audio-tour."

Father held his index-finger to his lips.

"Help," I said. "Somebody help me."

"Sshhh," Father said. "You're bothering people."

"I am not."

I stepped out of the cell and moved along the cell-row dragging my fingers lightly across the bars. Father was far behind me, one hand on his headphones, his face very concentrated and smooth. Father was a short man with short legs and short arms, narrow, stooped shoulders and a wide, oversized head. I knew then that there was nothing real in the real world. I touched an iron bar. I said aloud, "Taxidermy." I don't know why I said 'taxidermy' but I said it and a man who'd been inspecting a nearby wall moved quickly away, glancing wildly in my direction as he walked, nearly tripping over a black-haired toddler. I followed the man outside where the sun was a large red ball hanging loosely from little thin clouds. He stopped near a low fence on the edge of the hill overlooking San Francisco and the San Francisco Bay, one foot on a low rock, eyes half-closed. I moved very near the man. "Taxidermy," I said.

"Don't say that." The man turned toward me. He knotted his hands together in front of his chest and looked down at me over the tops of his fingers. "Please don't," he said.

"Why not?"

"It's terrible, terribly hollow. You know, empty. A death-word. I can't stand to hear it anymore. It's evocative of something." He emphasized the word 'evocative.' He held 'evocative' there in his mouth. "It's evocative," he said again. "It's like dead things."

"So what?" I hung my audio-tour headphones on the fence. "It sort of is dead things anyway, isn't it?"

"Listen, taxidermists only stuff pet cats and kittens and dogs anymore. Then these people put the pets on their walls and bookshelves and mantles, on nightstands next to beds or stacked, pyramided maybe, in closets or playrooms, next to the fireplace. Combing the fur on weekends, then just sitting there and watching their dead pets. It's really terrible. They just sit there, on weekends or whatever, drinking lemonade, and gazing at these stuffed things. Petting the pets. Combing the fur."

"But what if that's what they want to do?"

"I'm a taxidermist." He turned away. "I know what taxidermy is."

"You should stuff people," I said.

"What?"

"You should kill people and stuff them and put them in life-like poses in their own homes. Like a serial-killer. You could murder and stuff whole families and arrange them carefully in their homes. You know, life-size dioramas—like playing Monopoly or eating a home-cooked meal—meat-loaf, or fish-sticks—or arguing about what TV show to watch. You could be famous, the taxidermurderer."

"Why would I want that?"

"Why does anyone want anything?" I picked up my audio-tour head-phones and placed them on the taxidermist's head.

"Why'd you do that?"

"You ask too many questions—you're boring. I should smash you with a rock. I thought taxidermists were interesting probably with stories about gigantic bears and natural history museums, you know, dinosaurs or whatever. But you're just really boring." The taxidermist turned away and moved along the fence with little shuffling steps. I followed closely. "I'll follow you and tell people you're a serial-killer. About your serial-killer plan."

"Stop it."

"Kill people with kitchen knives, carefully skin their bodies and take the victim-skin and stuff it with sawdust and garbage, vegetable-scraps probably, empty beer-bottles, and sew it all together. Dress it up like real people and put them in your basement as pretend friends and lovers. Eat the organs probably. Cook and eat the organs, and serve them to your family, the organs and entrails and meat, with basil and parsley and chili-oil to disguise the taste."

The taxidermist moved away. "You're disgusting. You're terrible and terribly terrible or something, something."

I took a running step toward the taxidermist and stopped, poised on one foot. I imagined the taxidermist stuffing my body with sawdust and using a scalpel to make slow incisions along my belly, then hanging me from a pulley-system over a bathtub so my body-liquids would slowly drain into the bathtub and so my entrails and organs would flop out into the bathtub and dry there.

Father touched my shoulder. "What are you doing out here?"

"There was this taxidermist," I said. I told Father about the pulley-system and the incisions and stuffed families eating plastic dinners. Father watched a small square of my face, above and to the left of my left eye. He seemed to be slowly counting in his head. "Nothing," I said.

"I can't handle this anymore. You have to stop this shit, just tell the truth, no need to make shit up about taxidermists. Something terrible could happen. Something really terrible. Who would believe you? I need to know I can trust you. In an emergency, you could have dire information. Like a nuclear holocaust. We need to be able to know you're trustworthy, okay? Okay?"

"That's not true. That's not at all true."

Father shook his head slowly and I followed him down to the ship. We boarded the ship, leaned against the gunwale until it began to vibrate. The ship moved slowly into deep water. Father hugged me for a moment and together we watched San Francisco grow larger, Father's wide hand on my shoulder. The water below was gray and curved and I thought about swimming in that water, about lying there on my back, the sky clouded above. Father watched something above my head, but when I turned I saw nothing but open sea. "Everything's true all the time, right?" he said. "But I have to go to the bathroom to murder an orca. Three orcas probably. Total evisceration. That kind of death. Stay here, this could be dangerous." He moved past me toward the front of the ship. I followed, hiding behind mingling passengers, abandoned backpacks, low tables, plastic chairs. I was very small then. I wanted to drink a Pepsi. I wanted to ask Father for quarters for the soda-machine. Father was in front of me, his wide oversized head balancing strangely on his narrow neck, his little gray sweater hugging his narrow torso. If I asked him for quarters he might demand to know what they were for. I considered this as I followed. Father didn't approve of soda. He didn't approve of sugar, or syrup. The ship rocked a little with the waves and Father's legs and my legs absorbed the rocking and we moved weirdly, awkwardly forward. The ship moved smoothly, swiftly through the low waves. Finally, Father's hands grasped the gunwale and pulled on the gunwale until Father's body was perched on the gunwale and Father's face looked for a moment at my face until Father's body shivered slowly over the gunwale and disappeared silently beneath the ship.

SIXTEEN

"What's a gunwale?" I ask.

"Part of a boat," Grandfather answers.

"Change the channel," Erik says. "I hate this show."

We're watching CHiPs. Erik Estrada and Larry Wilcox are riding motorcycles through the foothills of the Siskiyous, side by side, pursuing a red Chevy Nova. There's cocaine in the Nova's ceiling panels. Erik is Erik and Erik's on television and also next to me. If Erik Estrada and Erik were the same Erik, would the TV implode? I imagine Erik and the television imploding: Erik stands next to the television. Erik and the television expand suddenly, then slowly contract toward a central point. The point pulls Erik-atoms and television-atoms individually, then in large atom-clumps until Erik and the television become the central point. Stepmother has set the scrapbook aside.

"I want to see more photos," Aaron says.

"All our photos were destroyed in a house-fire," I say. "Cameras too."

"They were not!" Stepmother says.

"She has Alzheimer's and senile-dementia," I say. "Everything was destroyed. The fire killed two kittens. I can't look at kittens anymore, not without weeping."

Grandfather begins to chuckle. "And my leg burnt off and I have a wooden leg." He grabs his leg and shakes it. "See, lifeless. When the heat clicks on I can't stop crying. I can't stand on decks. I can't go to hardware stores. Skill-saws terrify me. It's really terrible."

"Can I have the remote-control?" Erik asks.

"Anastasia started the fire," I say. "She was making Molotov cocktails in her bedroom. Anastasia was an anarchist, even in elementary school. She was terribly violent and devious. She made a shiv in metal-shop. Just sheet-metal, a little spot-welding. She sliced my arms while I slept. She drained the blood into little glass bottles and saved them under her bed, each one labeled with withdrawal date and time. The little glass blood-bottles burned in the fire though, and then there was nothing, no blood, no records, no Anastasia."

"What?" Stepmother asks.

Grandfather's laughing. "It's all true," he says. "Every part."

SEVENTEEN

Anastasia hid beneath her bed. Merna was at her boyfriend's house. I sat at the kitchen-table with Mother. We were drinking tall glasses of milk. Mother's hair was long and brown and soft and beautiful, and the hair was very thin and shiny and Mother had pulled it over her very slim shoulder. Mother looked at me with her eyes and her eyes were large green eye-shapes and her eyes blinked at a slower, stranger rate than mine. We sat together at the kitchen table with our hands on milk-glasses, carefully tipping the milk-glasses so the milk poured slowly into our mouths. I was little then and chubby and my hair was very dirty and tangled.

"Where's your father?" Mother said.

"I don't know."

"Did he say where he was going or when he'd be back when he left?"

"I think he went to work."

"Hah!" Mother finished her milk and slammed her milk-glass on the tabletop. "Hah!" she said again. She was leaning back in her chair.

"Are you taking me to school today?"

"I don't think you should go to school anymore, or I think your father should take you to school. I'll call him for you. Maybe ... did he give you a phone-number to call him at?"

"I don't think so." I tried not to look at Mother's face because it was a little wrinkled oval with sad eye-shaped eyes blinking slowly while the eyeballs moved wildly from one object to another.

"Let's go shopping," Mother said. "We'll go shopping and chat and be like friends, but I'm still your mother. Let's get dressed and go shopping. Get dressed and we'll go shopping? I'll take you, we'll go to the mall, we'll go shopping and we'll talk, and I'll buy you a soda and a piece of candy, no not candy, I'll buy you a soda and an ice-cream cone. We'll get fancy ice-cream cones with fudge and strawberries and cheesecake and we'll go shopping, just the two of us, and we'll talk and it'll be fun and touching and something to remember when I'm dead." Mother was a behavioral-psychologist. She worked at a university research facility with other psychologists and a thousand white mice and mazes and little white soundproof-rooms. She often told me about the white soundproof-rooms. "We keep the mice in there," she'd say. "I wish I had a room like that. I'd stay in that room at home. I'd take you with me to the soundproof-room and we could talk without other people talking and without sounds. No creaking floorboards or bird-calls, no pigeons, doves, seagulls, no dishwasher or refrigerator-engines or cars. There are noises everywhere and you can't stop the noises because the noises make waves in the air and the air particles move with the airwaves and our ears interpret the airwaves as sounds so the thing to do's have a little white soundproof-room and stay there until all you can hear is your body-sounds, like your heart and lungs, your pumping blood, your lungs holding air like a machine, you know? We'd go together and talk for a while and make the waves in the air and the only waves in the air would be our own airwaves. We would own them and they would be solitary." I thought about that while I watched Mother across the table. I wanted her to take me to the room, to feed then the mice, to put them in little cardboard mazes. "Get dressed," Mother said. "We're going shopping."

I wore my Halloween costume, a glittery pink dress and matching tiara. Mother drove slowly to the shopping-mall. I turned off the radio. Mother parked and we ran to the shopping-mall entrance and stood there, watching the people-swarms, the shop-facades. Hot Topic, See's. Kiosks with cell-phones, sunglasses, silver rings. "Come on!" Mother said. "Let's go to JC Penney." She took me to the fitting room, stuffed packages of socks and t-shirts and chocolates into my pink dress. Mother folded skirts and blouses and shoved them beneath her skirt and blouse. "Come on!" she said. We ran out to the parking-lot and laughed a lot. Mother opened the car-trunk and placed the blouses and skirts inside the trunk and had me place the socks and shirts and chocolates inside the trunk. We stacked them carefully, formed our own thing-grid. Rectangular, padded. Protected. "Good job!" she said. Mother held my hand. "Let's go to Sears!" Mother said. In the Sears dressing room, Mother hid wrenches, screwdrivers, and hammers beneath my pink dress. She hid neck-ties, belts, and cumberbunds beneath her skirt and blouse, and she held my hand and we ran swiftly outside to the parking-lot where the sky was a looming gray overcoat and where the black asphalt was wet with rain and dirt and dust. She opened the trunk and we placed our stuff in the trunk, arranged it, padding each delicate thing. "Now ice-cream!" Mother took me to a table in the food-court and I sat at the table and the table was cold and plastic and blue. "Wait here, at this table," Mother said. "I'll get the ice-cream. You want fudge right? Hot fudge? I know just the thing."

She walked slowly among the moving people and I watched her until I couldn't see her anymore. I sat at the table and watched the people move, thought how each person was a person somehow thinking unique thoughts. I saw an old woman with a plastic rain-bonnet pulled tightly to her head. "Hello," I said. "What's that?" I pointed at the rain-bonnet.

"Respect your elders," the woman answered.

"I do."

"You're an evil little thing aren't you?"

I looked at the old woman's eyes and the old woman's eyes were round and gray and motionless. "I am not," I said. "I am me," I said.

"You're a little bitch is what you are."

"My mother's here and I'll get my mother and she'll tell you," I said. My eyes looked for my mother.

The old woman moved her face close to my face. The face was very wrinkled and the mouth was a toothless black hole with a gray shriveled tongue. The tongue wiggled strangely at me. I tried to move away but the old woman's hand was on my neck. The hand gripped my neck like a handle. "You're a filthy murdering vile bitch," the old woman said. "If I were your mother I'd drown you in the bathtub like a kitten and I feed your dead kitten-body to the monkeys at the zoo if the monkeys at the zoo would eat it which they wouldn't, you know? Because you stink. You useless child thing robot bitch." The old woman pushed me and moved slowly away, her slippered feet shuffling over the white tile.

I searched for my mother, moving from table to table, peeking beneath the tables, around the chairs. I went to the Burger King counter and asked if anyone'd seen my mother. No one answered. The mall-lights snicked off and the shopping-mall was a dark, empty place. I ran to the door and out to the parking-lot, to the parking-space where Mother had parked but no car was there and no car was in the parking-lot and the parking-lot was an empty black thing with little empty lines and the sky was an empty black nothing. I traced some of the parking-spaces with my toe. There were no people, no cars, nothing, so I walked out onto the highway. I searched for a sidewalk but there was none. Only a narrow asphalt space beyond a white line. The wind was swift and cold. My house was somewhere and I tried to walk toward it. When cars drove nearby, I hid in the tall grass next to the highway. My arms and legs were scratched and bleeding and the little scratches itched. I imagined Mother's car as a great glowing beacon, very large and car-shaped sitting solidly on the horizon, a stone fortress, but mobile. I imagined my child-body approaching the beacon with little child-steps, my bloody scratches slowly healing, itch-less now, my dress clean and pressed, my tiara perched in my very clean very straight hair. Maybe the beacon was on a hilltop and I climbed the hill for three months or three years even, then sat cross-legged before the beacon and gently slept next to the beacon with my little dirty head resting on the little dirty tire. The beacon warm and glowing, my child-body within the glowing warmth.

EIGHTEEN

"In the war," Grandfather says, "We'd of made men out of two pissants like you."

"What war?" asks Erik.

"Oh, some war or other. I think I was a sergeant, but don't hold me to that. You know, I drove one of those jeeps, like on M*A*S*H, and it was boring. I gambled, cards mostly, had relations with the nurses, etc..."

Stepmother's preparing dinner. Aaron's somewhere. I'm sitting next to Erik on the couch, across from Grandfather who's sprawled in his easy-chair.

"Did you kill people?" I ask.

"Oh, I killed lots of things. I think I killed a water-buffalo."

"Oh."

"It's like this. Everything that's alive dies and so it's no big deal to kill a thing because it's natural. People don't kill things directly and so think killing's evil. It's not. Every person should kill something— start in elementary school. If I were President, I'd mandate that each kindergartner slaughter a live chicken the first day of school, then every year thereafter, first day of school, students would slaughter a larger animal. Rabbits, cats, mountain-goats, all the way up to senior year and a healthy goddamn bovine. This would take some planning and maybe you just have one fucking cow per home-room. I don't know, but America would be a better place if there was more killing and a more comprehensive understanding of death."

Aaron steps into the family-room, placing his cell-phone in its belt-holder. "Sorry to be a bother, but I have to get going."

"Where, why?" I imagine watching myself—my mouth flapping flag-like.

"I have a meeting downtown, real-estate deal. I'll pick you up later, maybe. Coffee?" Aaron looks from me to Erik.

"Can I come?" Erik says. "Want to ride in that Lexus a little more. Just hang out."

"Fine."

"What's your cell-phone number?" I ask. "What if I need to call? I can't call you if I don't have your number."

"Here." Aaron hands me his business card.

In the corner of the card's a line-drawing. It seems very mysterious and abstract—lines shooting out randomly from a blank center, and I can't imagine what form it's supposed to represent. I want the drawing to be a living thing like a beetle or a kitten, an antelope, but it's none of these. "What's this for?" I trace the drawing with my pinky and watch my pinky move jerkily with the lines.

"That's a W. That's my company's symbol." Aaron looks at Erik. "Ready?"

"Yeah."

"Very good, then."

I follow Aaron and Erik to the front-door and open the front-door and watch Aaron and Erik move steadily along the walkway to Aaron's Lexus. It's evening. The sky's clear. There's snow on the grass but the road-snow has melted. The roadside's lined with dirty slush. The neighborhood houses have many lights and the lights are many colors and the many-colored lights are bright and blinking and moving and the night's a cold, empty cavity with only colored lights and a thin, tragic wind. The lights move slightly, with the wind, and I want to touch them, to move close and let my hand arrange the lights around the trunk of my body and then to lie there, glowing in the street.

"How are you, really?" Grandfather asks. His hand's on my shoulder.

The Lexus's moving in the street.

"I'm a cavity."

"What?"

"Happy fucking birthday to me."

"Oh, to be young," Grandfather says. "I was young and then I was old. No big difference. Everything basically the same, except my knees, which hurt all the time, and I don't think they did that before, maybe. They could have hurt then. It's hard to say. Maybe I only now noticed the hurting." He patted his knee. "I think more now, probably. No, that's wrong. Now, I watch more television. That could be the same thing. I like the news. Watch the news every day, five times a day. The world's going to end sometime and I'll figure out when and how. I'll be the first." I follow Grandfather into the family-room. We sit on the sofa. "Do you know about the apocalypse?" Grandfather asks.

"Not really."

"It's bullshit but comforting bullshit." Grandfather groans and adjusts his legs with his hands. "I like to imagine a nuclear holocaust because a nuclear holocaust's probably the best kind of apocalypse. Nuclear holocausts have the most drama. There's the initial explosion, you know, mushroom cloud, extreme heat, gaudy casualty numbers. News-media panicking over wind direction, government response, etc... Will it rain? Who knows? People trampled or stomped trying to escape the flat dark cities, which would seem like death-traps. The inevitable retaliation, with the same two rounds of death and panic in other countries, Portugal, Belgium maybe, a thousand countries. Radiation burns. Radiation sickness. More bombs, more dead, more radiation, more panic. Praying and stuff. People becoming religious. Mass graves. Bodies burned. A very melodramatic end, I think."

"That doesn't sound comforting."

"Well." Grandfather watches television for a while. "I think it's comforting to know that things have an end, small scale, lives etc..., and also large scale, world, universe. It's good to know that things end completely. If things go on perpetually...it's impossible to imagine, makes me, people, everyone, I think, anxious and fearful. If a television show never ended it'd be creepy, scary, people wouldn't know what to do. Maybe television-destruction-derby, urban rioting, domestic violence, you know kitchen-knife stabbings. Women tossing boiling water on their husbands in the garage. Poor old grandmothers stumbling bloodily into the snow. So to with the world, I think."

"That's sad."

"Maybe."

"What about time?" I ask. "You know the passage of time."

Stepmother calls from the kitchen. Dinner's ready. Roast beef, mashed-potatoes.

"That's exactly it," Grandfather says.

We're walking to the kitchen.

"It's nice to know that even time has an end."

We sit at the kitchen-table, forming an equilateral triangle. Stepmother has arranged the plates and cutlery into their proper places. Steam rises from the sliced roast beef and it glistens in the light, reflects it, and the kitchen feels like a slick and slimy place. "What do you think about the apocalypse?" I say to my stepmother. "Are you for, or against?"

"Your sister's here," she answers. "She's just cleaning up now."

"What?"

"I called her and told her to come. It's your birthday after all."

Grandfather chuckles quietly. "It's not the end of the world," he says. "Watch out for that beef though. It's irradiated beef."

"Irradiated?"

"Got a discount from this guy in a white van. A white van discount. Was driving through the neighborhood with this truckload of beef, one of these cut-rate, 'somebody ordered it but they died' deals. Round steaks, T-bones, chuck steak, cube steak, flank steak, filet mignon, sirloin steak, ground-chuck, rib-eye, spare-ribs, everything. I asked him why it's so cheap and he says, 'radiation poisoning' and I say, 'I'm old anyway' so I bought it all for fifty bucks. Probably a whole cow in that goddamn freezer."

"Oh hush," Stepmother says.

She looks toward the hallway. "Here she is," she says.

My sister steps into the room and she's Merna. Merna's holding her hands in front of her stomach and her hair's like my hair but short and her eyes are like my eyes but large and round and her jeans are very tight and stylish and Merna's mouth's smiling a wide smile and I can see her teeth which are large and white and even. She moves in a slow-shuffling way and she sits between my stepmother and me. I move a little and we become a trapezoid-family. "Trapezoid," I say.

"What?" Merna says.

"Nothing bitch-face."

"Don't," Merna says.

"It's the same," I say.

There's meat between my sister and me.

"Everything's probably the same," Merna says.

NINETEEN

"Come on upstairs with me," Merna says. Dinner's finished and the plates are streaked with dirt and grease and there's a smell like stomach-acid.

"Why?"

"Come up on the roof with me. We'll sit on the roof. It's beautiful there."

"It's cold."

"You're my little sister, right?"

"I guess."

"Isn't it natural then, that you'd do something for me if I ask? It's okay though, if you don't want to."

"I know." I look at Merna's mouth and Merna's mouth moves and there's saliva, teeth, other things. I turn my body away from Merna. The air feels dense and long, somehow, and I think birthday thoughts. Grandfather's napping on the sofa. Stepmother's throwing dishes one by one into the trash compacter and laughing quietly alone.

"You're still pretty," Merna says. "Sometimes I imagine that you're doing very pretty very smart things, studying to be a marine-biologist, a physicist or something, sculpting important 'politically-charged' sculptures, collage-sculpting, from toy and food fragments. You create a new art movement called collage-sculpting, the cover of Time Magazine, art shows, minor critical success, some kind of website."

"Hmm."

"Come out on the roof so we can look at the constellations."

"I'm sorry I never called. I think I was probably busy." I don't know what to say. "You know, busy busy."

"Don't worry about it." Merna stands and walks toward the stairs. "Come on," she says over her shoulder. "I'm going out on the roof."

I follow Merna up the stairs and out her bedroom window. The roof's slippery and cold but we lay a thick fleece blanket over the snow. Lighted houses rise up along the hillside in succeeding tiers, the road snaking between them. The sky's clear and black and distant, and the stars are cold and strange. I try to find the constellations and wonder how you tell a constellation from anything else. I arrange the stars in different combinations. I want them to move. To spread into orderly grids, matrices. "What do you think about apocalypses?" I say to Merna. Apocalypse matrices. "Grandpa thinks apocalypses are comforting."

"I don't know," Merna says. Merna silently touches my hair, and leans back against the roof, resting her body on her elbows. "I think it's beautiful for an apocalypse to happen, probably proof of god or something. Proof that there's some real beginning to something. I don't know."

I think about the apocalypse, nuclear holocaust, general havoc and destruction, and I feel all at once like Grandfather's correct. It is comforting to know that things end. "But what about human suffering?" I ask. "Or at least physical pain?" I try to quantify the combined physical pain of each dying human during a worldwide apocalypse. It's not quantifiable, and instead I imagine slaughtering a small white kitten, a dozen white kittens, carefully cutting small kitten-pieces and placing the kitten-pieces in a large silver bowl, a billion kitten-pieces from a million kittens. Worldwide human suffering must be like that, incremental and ongoing.

"I don't know," Merna says. "If I was god I'd arrange a beautiful apocalypse with rivers of blood and fire, evenly spaced explosions, rhythmical somehow, and from a great height, I'd arrange the corpses into complicated patterns, chaotic and touching patterns, flower-like, familial, and every dead body would touch another dead body, and it would cover everything up and then it would snow for a while, I think."

"Snow," I say.

We don't talk much after that. I know that any apocalypse would begin in a parking-lot. I want to tell Merna but I don't. When we were small, Merna and I played the apocalypse-game. Early Saturday mornings. We searched the house for every doll and stuffed-bear, every toy animal—dolphins, penguins, my little cabbage-patch girl—and scattered them, each one touching another, radiating around a central point as though a bomb had tossed their toy-bodies about and we sat carefully between the bodies and lamented them. "It's sad," Merna would say each time. I would wait a moment before answering. "It's sad but it's just stuff that happens. The animals die. I saw it before on TV." I would search for more stuffed-animals to arrange in the blast zone. I would throw pillows among them like concrete shrapnel. Merna would topple tables and nightstands, our little plastic lamp. We would pretend we were paramedics. Try and fail to resuscitate. Apply chest compressions to the penguins. Telephone defibrillator. "Clear." Dispel the gathering crowds with megaphones. Merna would pronounce time of death, then help gather and remove the bodies from the bomb-site. Merna would say a little sermon in our bedroom. I would sit in the audience, then transform into the grave-digger. I would bury the dead beneath red and gray fleece-blankets, sheets, old pink sweaters.

"Do you ever want to eat yourself?" I ask.

"What do you mean?"

"I don't know exactly. Sometimes I'm hungry, but not hungry and I think I should slowly eat myself and disappear inside myself. I think about starting with my abdomen. Making a little cavity with a kitchen-knife or a potato-peeler, a melon-baller. Baking my little abdomen balls in garlic or something, or maybe a soup, a nice me-soup with parsley."

"I've never thought that."

"Yeah?" I open my cell-phone and scroll through my cell-phone address-book. I text-message Erik. I type, 'Apocalypse death warrant.'

"What're you doing?" my sister asks.

"Nothing." I text-message Aaron. I type, 'I eat myself, self, all teeth and stuff.' I say, "Just texting." I want Aaron and Erik to text me back. To pick me up, drive me around for a while, then kill me and roast me in a barrel-fire. Serve my roast-body to lonely homeless men with wide pocketed jackets. In New Mexico maybe, in a parking-lot full of Jolly-Rogers. But Aaron and Erik don't text me. I put my cell-phone slowly away. Snow falls in a loose and dangly way and there's space between each snowflake and I avoid the snowflakes near my face.

I could remain untouched by snow, if I wanted.

"Do you remember that little dog, Ana, the neighbor's dog?"

"No." But I do remember her and I can see her little black eyes in her little narrow face and her thin brown shoulders and her black spiked collar with its jingling nametag.

"We used to take her for walks to the park, you know, fetch and stuff in the street."

"Hmm."

"Little Ana's dead," Merna pauses. "She's in my trunk. I sort of hit her. I was thinking about it. Thinking about burying her, or something. Would you cook her? Cook a dog."

"I don't know."

"Dogs are like people, aren't they? Somehow. Do dogs think? Maybe dogs think smell-thoughts."

"Why'd you hit her?" I watch a white Volvo wagon move carefully along the road.

"It was an accident."

"You did it on purpose. You swerved, right?"

"No, I'd never."

I wonder what I'd never do. "I know, probably. It's cold in your trunk. Should we do something with the dog?"

"I don't know."

My cell-phone plays a little song.

"Don't answer it," Merna says. "We're here now. Together. Let's just sit here." Merna watches me holding my phone. "You really don't have to answer it. It's late. We'll just sort of lay here awhile, on the blanket. Call back later. Let them leave a message."

I look down at my cell-phone, the folding smallness of it, how its slim rectangular shape smoothly fits in my palm, un-living and inhuman, gray and antenna-less, and I begin to think of it as a robot-ear, my ear-replacement. The beginning, finally, of a newer, better, robot-me. "I'm sorry," I say. I open the cell-phone.

TWENTY

"Meet us at Highland Ice Arena," Erik says. His voice is light and static-y. "We're going ice-skating." In my brain, I hear Erik whispering 'I'm Todd' and feel confused.

"It's closed. All melted," I answer. "We don't have ice-skates. Anyway, I don't know how."

"Who is it?" Merna asks. "What's it want?"

"Ice-skating. They want to go ice-skating."

There's a birch screech-owl screwed to the roof and with its owl-face it stares down on the front-yard, all fierce eyebrows and violent curved beak. I touch the rough owl-body and think about shredded starlings or fruit bats.

"Just meet us there," Erik says. "Aaron's got the keys. We'll use the rental-skates and I'll drive the zamboni. It'll be cool."

"Who?" Merna asks.

"We can play broom-hockey or something. We can body-check. I've never body-checked before. Get pads from the pro-shop."

I put my hand over the cell-phone speaker. "My stupid little lovers," I say to Merna.

"Listen," Erik says. "We're breaking in. Bet that gets you excited. We'll commit unspeakable, bloody crimes. We'll murder a thousand goldfish. I've already kidnapped and slaughtered that black sheep, Bobo, you know, high school mascot and stuff. Who knows what I'll do next? Eat a corndog? Revolutionary war? Could be anything" Erik's laughing, and distantly I can hear Aaron laughing. "Bring your bathing suit and a hockey-puck. It's celebration time."

I turn off my cell-phone. "We're going ice-skating I guess."

"I'll drive."

We pass Grandfather on the way out. He sits quietly in the darkened family-room. "It's cold in here," he says.

"Turn the heat up," Merna answers.

"Heat's not the problem. It's the cold. I've catalogued it—this is the coldest day in the last five-hundred years, scientific fact, has to do with the spin of the earth, which is slowing, because of fat people. Too many morbidly obese people gathered in one place. It's the opposite of centripetal force." Merna and I are near the front door, our hands both reaching for the doorknob momentarily, and then recoiling as the hands collide. Grandfather's chuckling. "The earth has a hernia and wants to sleep, like I want to sleep."

"Herniated earth," I mumble.

"Where's Grandma?" Merna asks. She opens the front door and cold air rushes in. "Shouldn't you be in bed or something?"

"I don't sleep anymore. Waste of time. I decided, maybe four years ago, no more sleep. And stuck to it. I have these visions. Like a constant vision-quest. Like Nostradamus. Prescience, I have prescience. Helps when I go to the horse-track, the grocery-store."

I want suddenly to go to the horse-track with Grandfather. I'd wear a baseball cap, the brim pulled low. Grandfather in a panama hat.

"We'll be back later," Merna says.

Merna's Honda's red and very narrow. We sit close, shoulders almost touching, and the windshield's large, bubble-like and reflects Merna and me. I watch our thin reflected faces as the Honda drifts from streetlight to streetlight. Outside, it's very dark and cold and a stiff wind shakes the car. The moon's distant and the sky's open and cotton-y. I feel the Honda slipping and worry that it'll slip into the sky somehow. A controlled skid. New Mexico. Skidding from sky to parking-lot, dirty slush everywhere. Bill Murray waiting with the Jolly-Roger, in Lisbon, sadly slumped over a low curb. American flag draped over his shoulders. I dreamed that once, terribly, and the memory of the dream makes me sweat a little.

"What kind of dog is it?"

"I don't know." Merna frowns. "The kind in a garbage-bag." I want to open the trunk, to see the garbage-bag there, arranged carefully between tool boxes, disaster survival-kits, a crate of bottled water. The light above. Would the garbage-bag be lumpy in that light? Merna's hands are very pale. She continues, "Didn't mean to hit her. Just turned my head for a second, and she's there and there's a sound, a bark, then no sound. Completely silent. Who lets invisible dogs roam free, at night no less? I'm no murderer. Just an accident. I just scooped her in the bag. Didn't know what to do, what I was supposed to do."

"I could be a murderer," I say quietly. In the world where I'm a famous murderer, I stand near a tree full of screech-owls. Horrible curved beaks, a warbling. I call the President on my cell-phone. It's very quiet.

"What'd you say?"

"I said you don't have to convince anyone."

"Do you think they'll be pissed, say I hit her purposely, call the Police?"

"Who?"

"Them. Mindy and Matthew, I think. They're old, ancient. They could've forgotten the dog by now. Maybe that's why she was walking out in the dark. Old people often forget things, which is why it's so great to be old. But they could sue me or something, if they somehow remembered."

"Maybe," I say. "Take you to People's Court or whatever."

"You think so?"

"They're probably searching for the dog right now." I look at Merna and Merna's face is slim and heart-shaped and her skin's smooth and soft-looking. Her hair's arranged neatly in a bun and pinned in place and Merna's shirt's very balanced and she's beautiful and professional and bright. "Mindy's probably crying. Crying and looking for her little black dog and Matthew's angry, punching his kitchen wall repeatedly." I picture the wall. It's red. There are rhododendrons. "He promised to never let Mindy cry but he's powerless now, probably powerless for the first time and he's angry and hurt, like his chest is bubbling kind of, with the anger, and he's sweating, and the worst part is that he doesn't know why or how the dog disappeared. He has no revenge. His fists are bleeding, little long drops of it. There are asymmetrical holes in the drywall and Matthew and Mindy are probably inconsolable so they go upstairs to the study with the abandoned-barn-paintings and the empty bookcase. And they pull the matching antique shotguns from above the mantle, load them with buckshot, brace them against the floor, and blast themselves, one by one, through the mouth." I say all this staring straight ahead, then turn to Merna.

"Thanks a lot." Merna drums the steering-wheel lightly. "I didn't ever want to kill anything."

We're waiting at an empty intersection. The light's red. Just ahead, the ice arena waits, a flat-roofed rectangle with wide glass doors and a wall of tall scratched windows. All the windows are dark.

"What time is it?" I ask.

"Ten-fifteen."

"Park the car," I say. I think the words, ice-flag Lisbon, then wonder what they mean and smile nervously. "Ice arena," I say. Merna, Anastasia, and I were here once. Highland Ice Arena. Dozens of bright red holiday-sweaters skated distantly. Us three in matching blue snow-parkas, large floppy hoods. The floors, walls, even the ice seemed knit together from some uncommon fiber, something simultaneously hard and soft and each time I stepped forward the floor recoiled a little and I bounced slightly and each wall was very far from every other wall. I felt unbalanced and dizzy. Merna chose figure-skates. Anastasia, hockey-skates. Anastasia disappeared only to reappear moments later with a freshly taped hockey-stick. I showed my little brown ticket and asked for skates, any skates. The man gave me tiny white ones with rusty blades. I tried to wipe them clean, used my saliva. Nothing changed. We laced up on the narrow wood bench, left our shoes beneath it, and waddled slowly, hand in hand, toward the ice. The ice was very clear and slick and wet and we stepped onto it and slid and pushed and slid. "Don't let me fall," I said. "I don't want to fall. I don't want people laughing at me if I fall. I don't want

96

people laughing at me hurting myself when I fall."

Merna spun and moved off. "You'll be fine," she said. Merna skated backward, her head turned over her left shoulder, neatly avoiding a little black-haired boy dragging his mother behind him, then leapt into the air and spun a full circle.

I looked down at Anastasia and held Anastasia's hand and touched Anastasia's hair which was soft and black and shoulder-length. "You're a good skater," I said.

"Oh," Anastasia said. Anastasia pushed off, holding her hockey-stick high. "I'm taking lessons. I can skate backward too and I can stop without crashing." She demonstrated. "Here comes Merna!" she said. Merna slapped my cheeks, one two, as she skated by. Anastasia was laughing and I watched Anastasia's mouth move with the laughs and expose her little white teeth and her little pink tongue. I thought about things the tongue might say. Anastasia bumped me. "It's easy," she yelled, laughing. I wobbled and slid sideways and looked down. My skates were loose and white and the skate-blades wobbled and shook as I crumpled slowly to the ice. I spread out and slid and looked up at a fat woman in a Christmas sweater moving slowly, inexorably toward me. I pulled my pieces into a little ball, but too late. The fat woman skated over my pinky-finger and my pinky-finger was on the ice with the blood and water and I screamed as the fat woman toppled slowly onto me, crushing me. I reached for my pinky-finger but it slid, spinning, away and people skated around my pinky-finger until my pinky-finger disappeared. I cried quietly to myself and said, "My finger, my finger, my finger," until the fat woman rolled off, apologizing, and skated shamelessly away.

TWENTY-ONE

I open and close my hand and inspect my fingers. I inspect both
hands. I look through my fingers at Erik who's leaning against
Merna's Honda.

"Help me get her," Merna says. She opens her trunk.

The black garbage-bag's tied in a ball-like knot, stuffed between a
red plastic toolbox and a blue X-shaped tire-iron. The tire-iron seems
wonderfully balanced and solid and my fingers touch the tire-iron's cool
metal and trace the tire-iron's smooth ridges. We each grab a double-
handful of garbage-bag and lift, and just before Merna slams her trunk
shut I snag the tire-iron.

"Where's Aaron?" I ask.

"Inside," Erik says. "I'm driving the zamboni. It's all me."

"Carry this," I say. Merna and I toss the garbage-bag to Erik.

"What's in here?" Erik asks.

"Bathing suits," I say.

"Bathing armor, or something? Fucking chain-mail."

Inside the ice is floodlighted. Everything else is dark. Erik runs
ahead and hops the low white wall, dropping the garbage-bag mid-
jump. Erik and the bag hit the ice then slide tangentially. Merna and I
take skates from the rental-stand and put them on. We hobble together

to the low white wall. I side-arm the tire-iron and watch it skim toward the garbage-bag.

"Did she just move?" Merna asks, her eyes fixed on the garbage-bag.

"I don't know."

The garbage-bag tumbles sideways, blob-like and amorphous, then folds and flutters and bubbles. We're all watching it. I imagine the little dog moving with a mouthful of fingers, a finger-pile. Choking now in the garbage-bag.

"What the fuck is that?" Aaron says.

"How was your meeting?" I say.

"Why'd you bring a tire-iron?" Erik's slowly scratching his elbow. His eyes are narrow and unfocused, his lips trembling slightly.

"It's not a tire-iron," I say. "My new pet. We share an uncommon bond."

Nobody says anything.

"Uncommon bond," I say.

"No really, what's in the bag?" Aaron's eyes are very wide and round and I imagine holding them, or stacking the eyes on a pile of fingers—a bed of interlaced fingers, of ears, turned up to forever face a distant ceiling. To face gray acoustic ceiling-tiles. There's a parking-lot full of fingers. We can arrange them on a blanket in New Mexico and sell them. Raise money for the steamship tickets to Lisbon. "Fucking freaky," Aaron's saying. "Like a blob, an ice-blob, a gremlin or something." Aaron moves to the garbage-bag and holds it. The garbage-bag struggles against his hands, but the hands hold it firmly. "Warm," he says. "It's very warm. What if I spill water on it? What would happen then?" We could live in the garbage-bag. Make tents, find some abandoned plain in Alaska and trap antelope or something. I want to say this aloud, to talk about icy beaches and garbage-bags and fingers. Aaron tears a little hole and the dog erupts from the hole and bounds off Aaron's leg barking and spitting and snapping its jaws which are wide and shiny. "Fuck," Aaron says. "Fuck," Aaron says again. He dodges and slips. Waves his arms.

"She's alive," Merna says.

The dog shoots across the ice, bumping the walls then redirecting herself along sudden tangents. We scatter to avoid her, and her barks and howls are long and high-pitched. She's a solid black shape with a wet mouth and wet claws and little dangerous white teeth, and little clear globules of saliva that tremble on the tips of her teeth and from her thin black lips. Erik moves toward her, the blue tire-iron hanging loosely from his hand. "I'll get it," he says. Erik corners her near the front wall and lunges with the tire-iron. There's a crack and a ringing. The tire-iron bounces over the wall. "Shit!" Erik holds his elbow sort of desperately.

"Save the dog!" Merna says. "Shit, she's alive."

"I've got it." Erik's moving. Erik's skating flat-footed toward the dog with a large round-mouthed smile. "Here doggie," he says. "Calm doggie."

"We have to kill it," I say. "Look at those teeth." Aaron and I are sitting in the zamboni.

Erik scoops her up and pets her and nuzzles her with his face.

"Drop the dog," I say. "I'm going to smash it." I'm pulling zamboni levers. I'm turning wheels.

"It's a nice dog." Erik holds the dog high. "See, just didn't want to be in a plastic-bag. Most living things don't want to be in plastic-bags. That's like a standard principle."

"We have to kill the dog," I say. "That dog bit me once. With Merna—it was July, and this stupid stupid dog came running leash-less, without a collar. I tried to pet her little head and then it opened its jaws and snapped them over my arm, tore my goddamn arm and my arm-muscles and there was blood, okay. Lots of fucking blood. Everywhere. Blood fucking everywhere."

"It was probably stuck in a plastic-bag for a while. That's what I'd do if I were stuck in a plastic-bag."

"She's lying," Merna says. "Save the dog, okay."

"Really," Erik says. "I'd do that if I were stuck in a plastic bag. It might depend on how long."

"Be quiet," I say. Finger.

"You're being dramatic," Merna says. "She was a thespian, you know, in high-school."

"Doesn't matter," Aaron says. "It's only a dog."

"She was Lady Macbeth."

"I want that dog dead," I say. "It's a terribly violent dog and it deserves to die here on the ice and then to be abandoned, maybe tied, you know, spread-eagled to the wall with little cursive-like trails of blood on the ice or we could tie its little dead carcass to the zamboni like it's driving the zamboni in a cute way—like a calendar—and it could wear a little baseball-hat and sports-jersey, a butterfly-knife stuck in its eye." I hop down from the zamboni. Erik holds the dog away from me. "I won't hurt it yet," I say. "This will take planning."

"Hey?" It's a man's voice. There's a rustling and a creaking. "Who the fuck's there?"

"Shit," Aaron whispers. "Hide."

The dog barks. We all crouch behind the white half-wall except Erik. Erik stands silently with the dog in his arms. "Drop the dog and hide," I whisper. "Go."

"I can't," Erik says. "Don't want her to die, not yet." Erik stands there, the dog quiet in his arms.

Aaron's hunched next to me and he smiles then sneaks along the wall, holding his body low. Aaron places his finger over his lips, then whispers the word, "Flank," and I wonder what he means. I imagine flank-steak and then flack. What's flack? I think.

A flashlight's light appears and then a security-guard with a security-guard-uniform and a security-guard-hat and a security-guard-belt with a security-guard-radio and a security-guard-baton and he approaches with his security-guard-walk. He stares at Erik and the dog and the zamboni. "You know," he says. "This ice-skating rink's closed." He steps onto the ice through the wide break in the wall.

"Um," says Erik. "I lost my dog. She went in here and I followed her in, see." Erik holds the dog forward. "Probably a case of mistaken identity. I think. Just a mistake."

The security-guard holds his radio. "Somebody jimmied the lock. You jimmy the lock?"

"Jimmy? Jimmy's a name."

"You just stand there and shut the fuck up." He stares down at his radio and moves his hand near his baton. "What's your goddamn name?"

Aaron appears behind the security-guard. "Good evening sir," Aaron says politely. Aaron's holding the blue tire-iron behind his back and Aaron's smiling a wide smile with his little mouth. Aaron's eyes are wide and Aaron's fingers are thin and bent, the tire-iron dangling there and pale in the floodlights. I imagine what it would be like to hold the tire-iron as Aaron holds the tire-iron, thinly, with my own fingers. "I'm sorry, but you'll be okay. Everything's okay." Aaron raises the tire-iron up and swiftly brings it down on the security-guard-head and the tire-iron recoils from the security-guard-head and stays there in Aaron's fingers. There should've been a sound but I don't know what the sound should've been. There's blood and silence and the security-guard-body tumbles forward and becomes a lumpy uniformed shape. I'm not moving and I wonder why I'm not moving. "It'll be okay probably," Aaron says to the security-guard-body. Aaron pushes the body with his foot. "Nothing bad can ever really happen."

TWENTY-TWO

This isn't the first time I've seen a man hit with a tire-iron. Maybe. I picture other men, dark haired, naked—other tire-irons, blue, flashing in fluorescent-light or dulled by bloodstains, or oil, dirt, something. The blood, the man. The dog and the zamboni. Ice. The stark and flat floodlights. My little hands pale and cold. I stand next to Merna and touch Merna's hand and Merna touches my hand. The dog's licking the security-guard. Our hands are soft and small. I imagine them holding carefully magazines in an airport lounge. Jetplanes to Fairbanks, Lisbon, Albuquerque. "Help me tie him," Aaron says. He pauses, his eyes darting around the rink. "To the zamboni." Aaron wipes blood from Aaron's face. Bill Murray steering slowly a twin-engine Cessna. Grandfather the copilot.

"Okay," says Erik. "Okay?"

"Why'd he do that?" Merna says.

"What?"

"Why'd he hit him?"

Bill Murray hammering the controls, holding the radio, Grandfather's hand on his shoulder, the sound of ice in a glass, a bottle of Stolichnaya. Grandfather, silently mouthing, "Albuquerque." Aaron and Erik dragging the security-guard to the zamboni. Blood smears in a little trail behind them. If I were the security-guard. My little blood trail. My hand loosely cupping the air.

"Why did he?" Merna says.

I sit on a nearby bench and remove my ice-skates. I think about Merna's question, imagine a gray hallway with long flickering fluorescent-lights, paneled, surrounded by white acoustic ceiling-tiles. I'm in the middle of the hallway and even if I walk fifteen miles I'm always in the middle of the hallway. "I think," I say. Merna's eyes are wet and green and I want suddenly to have round green eyes, glittering eyes, like Merna's. I hate brown eyes. I imagine removing my own brown eyes and replacing them with green ones. Specially made glass eyes. Where would I get them? An optometrist. Bill Murray's an optometrist in New Mexico. Watching a mirror. Photographing the mirror me. Holding in his hand a lighted ophthalmoscope. Flipping the light off, then on again. "Would I see other things?" I say.

Merna seems confused. "What do you mean?"

"I think," I say, then, "optometry." I throw my ice-skates toward the front counter. The carpet's worn, shredded to the concrete in some places. The skates lean against a chipped blue bench. I begin again. "Every living thing's supposed to be tied up sometime, I think. Maybe just once. Aaron and Erik sort of know this instinctually and they're tying him because he's supposed to be tied and also everything should be hit once, hit with a tire-iron. See, this security-guard's never been hit with a tire-iron. He's lived a wonderful life with daughters, a wife, two wives and a girlfriend, or a boyfriend. He's been mostly happy with a thousand friends, high-school diplomas, so Aaron hit him with the tire-iron because it was a sort of fate. Maybe contrast for his happy security-guard life, like god's hand or something or maybe just one tiny part of god's will or, fate's...will, because everything happens sometime, for better contrast." I try to imagine everything happening sometime and it's patterned and regimented—each action's ranked and uniformed and I imagine a gigantic vein-y hand moving individual actions on an electronic grid. Bill Murray's hand. Bill Murray rubbing his temples, whispering, "Don't say thoughts," emphatically. I concentrate on the hand's monstrous fingernails which are dirty and long with jagged tips. "Fingernail," I say. "Maybe. Fingertips. New Mexico."

"They're tying his hands to the steering-wheel."

"I'm getting my shoes," I say. "I need my shoes." I stand.

"Um." Merna's following me.

"People should probably always walk barefoot. Shoes are inhuman. If shoes were in your lungs, for example, doctors would surgically remove the shoes. They'd be in the way. You'd have to cut them out..."

"Okay?"

"Why do you wear shoes, then?"

"Don't know. Cold. The cold."

I put my feet into my shoes and tie the shoelaces. "I'm sorry," I say to Merna. "I didn't mean to bring you somewhere where people are getting hit with tire-irons."

"Um."

"What are they doing? Can you see? I don't want to look."

Merna moves to the wide glass partition, puts her hand flat against it, and leans forward. "They're at the zamboni," she says.

"Your kitten," I say.

"What?"

"I'm sorry about throwing your kitten."

"Hmm." Merna sits next to me. Looks at my feet. Her foot touches my foot. "I haven't told you yet, but I have to tell you, okay? I have to tell you now." Merna's hair's neatly tied and Merna's arms seem very thin and long and the arms move fluidly and touch my shoulder. "It's important, okay. Just, okay?"

"You're only a little older than me now." My hands are on my lap. My hands are my lap. "Every year the amount your older gets smaller, I mean the percentage of years, until someday we'll be practically the same age, live together probably in some condo-compound. We'll be forgetful, with nurses and doctors, and we'll have dementia or something, a recreation room with Monopoly."

"Listen," Merna says. Her hands are holding her hands. "I took one of those tests and I'm pregnant, I mean, Noah gave me test at the hospital. We're having twins. I don't know the sex or whatever. They're tiny. They almost don't exist. I want you to help me have them, to be in the delivery-room with me, you know videotape it, to do something there with me. Help me name them. I don't know what name's a good name."

"You don't look pregnant."

"Only like six weeks. Had an ultrasound yesterday."

"You could probably still abort them if you wanted," I say. "You could stop it now."

"Why would I do that?"

"I don't know."

Merna touches her stomach. "I don't know how people can abort anything."

"It's what people should do because people make more people and there's already billions of people, with tire-irons, ice-skates, and they're making people. The world's a gigantic people-making machine, like automated, factory-thing, and somebody has to stop it. Things'll never end, not until people stop appearing from the little people-machines. It's impossible and painful, the duplication, people going on forever, reproducing forever until forever's really forever. Think about forever. As a hallway. Where is it? Things are supposed to stop and start, you know. Stop and start."

"Stop being weird. You're always weird." Merna's face is tight and closed.

I find that I'm touching lightly a lock of Merna's hair. I stand. "They're coming. The zamboni's moving."

"Be happy for me."

The zamboni's circling, resurfacing the ice, but very slowly—a wounded zamboni. Bill Murray chucking cherry trees in front of the zamboni. New Mexico or Lisbon. Bill Murray holding slowly the hand of an orphan boy. I look at Merna's forehead and the forehead's small and curved. "Wounded zamboni."

Merna touches my shoulder. "You're normal, just be normal."

"It starts with kittens, probably. It starts."

TWENTY-THREE

"You're probably normal, be normal," Merna said.

I was clutching my backpack to my chest. We were in the kitchen waiting to leave.

"Do not speak to me unless I speak first. People will know you're my sister already. It'll be obvious, but we won't talk about it, okay? We can pretend it's not true mostly, like we're strangers. You should have a cover story. Do you have a cover story? You're from somewhere else, Alaska maybe. You're always cold. You're from Fairbanks. You don't know me."

"But you're my sister."

"Learn to live ambiguously," Merna said. "You'll be happier and after a while we can have lunch together at the AM/PM, maybe winter quarter."

Grandmother handed me my lunch. "You've got fresh fruit," she said. "Fresh fruit's important, so eat it carefully. There are no preservatives. Preservatives are pretty much evil so it's important to not eat them. You understand, don't you? About freshness."

"I'll buy you a hotdog sometime." Merna made a blank face. "A corndog."

I opened my lunch bag and looked at my banana and my little green grapes.

"I'm driving with my friends, to school, okay?" Merna said. "We're driving in a car."

I set my lunch-bag on the kitchen-table and leaned against the kitchen-counter. The cabinets were solid walnut. I traced the cabinet-knob with my fingertip. I wanted then for Grandmother and Merna to leave, together perhaps, to pile into the Cadillac, push it rolling downhill, curving, the windows wide and blank, the sky open and very nearby. In New Mexico maybe. In my mind, I was often in New Mexico.

"Don't worry," Grandmother said. "Don'll drive you to school. He'll be back in a second. Just getting gas."

"Good luck," Merna said. "You'll probably need it." She disappeared.

"I have leukemia," I said to Grandmother. "I have leukemia and nobody's telling me. Just tell me. I'll freak out maybe, run around naked at the grocery-store, throw apples at bag-boys or something." Grandmother was laughing. "People with leukemia shouldn't go to school, right? People with leukemia should stay in bed all day, drink condensed chicken-broth, watch television, or stare sadly out the window as little children play hopscotch, ponder how a person with leukemia could be playing hopscotch if only leukemia wasn't slowly killing my blood."

"You're too old for hopscotch."

"You're too old for hopscotch," I repeated. "You're too old for leukemia."

"Here's Don."

Outside the kitchen-window I saw the wide white Cadillac slowly stop. The windshield was gigantic and wide and slightly tinted. Grandfather was only a dark rounded lump behind it.

"Go on. Take your lunch," Grandmother said.

"Leukemia," I said. "Leukemia, kemia." Grandmother disappeared so I shrugged and walked outside where my breath was foggy and wet. Grandfather was leaning with his arms crossed against the Cadillac. His eyes were wide and blue and rheumy and half-closed.

"This car's old," Grandfather said as I approached. "Doesn't have power-windows or anything, but the thing I like to do is pull up next to somebody and open my window very evenly so that the window seems like a power-window. I emit a low buzzing from the corner of my mouth. You have to do the sound." Grandfather demonstrated. "Go ahead, get in." We sat in the car. "Try it," he said. "Open your power-window."

"I can't. I have leukemia."

"Shit. That's terrible."

"My blood-cells are like a bunch of pyramid-shaped tumors with jagged little ridges that scratch my capillaries and vessels and stuff and I bleed internally and at every moment there's this jagged tumor-blood in my mouth. I can taste it right now. I taste it when I'm sleeping."

"That's nothing," Grandfather said. "Just before I was shipped off to Iwojima the FBI injected glass fragments into my arm to make me 'indestructible'."

"Oh?" I said. "I like stained-glass. Was it stained-glass?"

"I said to this FBI guy, 'You know, glass is hardly indestructible. I break glass all the time. It's the weekend pastime in Los Lunas. We get the gang together with baseball bats and walk down Main Street and smash every window, mirror, and streetlight within say a one-hundred foot radius, and we measure it carefully from a pre-chosen point, to make it official.' So the FBI agent says, 'This is special alien-glass, a Russian/alien technology, bullets, shrapnel, anything'll just bounce off you, sort of a force-field.' 'No shit?' I said. He assured me, showed me a couple graphs and an introductory film, kind of like a VD film, but about the glass. He was lying though. That Russian/alien-glass shredded my veins and stomach. Couldn't drink whiskey anymore. Some German shot my thigh right off. Now I have this limp. Didn't even dive for cover. I was so confident."

"Goddamn FBI," I said.

"I spent the war in a hospital with twenty-three other soldiers, all with the Russian/alien-glass in their blood and then the FBI agents gave us leukemia. 'Only way to kill the alien-glass,' they said. A lot of us died but I didn't, not then anyway."

"I wonder if my leukemia's your military leukemia passed genetically to me."

"Do you have glass veins?"

"I don't think so."

"Probably not, then."

The Cadillac was idling at a stoplight. In the next car an old woman with very tall very round white hair and narrow eyeglasses paged through a copy of Guns & Ammo. She was concentrated and serious as though between the shotguns and crossbows was an important word or phrase, some vital clue that would, finally, define her current role. The old woman spit into her Guns & Ammo and hammered her steering-wheel with it, then tossed it over her shoulder into the backseat. She turned and glared at me with her little eyeglassed eyes.

"What's life for?" I asked Grandfather.

"Conspiracy," he answered. "It's all a conspiracy. Christmas, for example."

"I always thought so."

"They want you to think it's one thing when it's really another thing."

"Who?"

"Oh, them." Grandfather released the brake and began, slowly, to drive forward. He kept the Cadillac very far to the right so we were very close to the old woman with Guns & Ammo and I could see her big wrinkled eyes which were lined with little red veins and capillaries. I imagined a crossbow, the woman holding it, her hands shaking. Grandfather parked in front of the school. I wondered about the Guns & Ammo women, about her crossbow. Taking aim then at a cow in an open field. Cyclone-fencing. I didn't know what cyclone-fencing was. The school was an eight-story brick fortress with iron-gates bolted over each window and a wide swinging double-door beneath a curved stained-glass window with little white doves and thick purple air.

I held my backpack tightly to my chest and said to Grandfather, "I'm going to do something sometime because."

"Like what?"

"I have no idea." I stepped onto the sidewalk and adjusted my backpack. I smiled down at Grandfather and Grandfather was very small and wrinkled. His body moved in little rapid shivers and when he smiled, his eyes moved in a wrinkled way. I felt suddenly very old, as though with my thin little hands I'd reached carefully into Grandfather's chest and took hold of something, which I then placed in my mouth. "I'll probably destroy the human race," I said. I wanted to be older than Grandfather, to be Grandfather's father and to look carefully every day at my own perfect wrinkles. "I'll probably kill everything," I said.

TWENTY-FOUR

"It starts with kittens." Merna doesn't hear me. Merna's watching the zamboni, carefully holding her flat stomach. I stand next to Merna, lightly touch Merna's shoulder. Bill Murray kittens in a basket. Door to door. Black suit, pink tie. The zamboni circles. The dog chases it. Aaron and Erik have left the ice and the ice's empty now except for the little dog and the zamboni, the security-guard tied to the zamboni, his head flopping as the zamboni lurches through a turn. The ice is very wet and the dog's sliding a little and weaving, barking short high-pitched barks that echo cavernously. It occurs to me that dogs don't have flags, don't sell them on blankets in parking-lots. Aaron and Erik are standing silently behind us, their faces expressionless.

"He's okay," Aaron says.

"He's not dead," Erik says. "Just looked bad. Just a little blood, but nothing major. I've had worse."

"Who?" I ask.

"The security-guard." Aaron points at the zamboni. "We didn't tie him too tight, just shoelaces anyway. He'll escape when it's important."

"What if he crashes?"

"We tied the wheel down so it'll keep circling." Aaron's chuckling. "Circle, circle," he says.

"The dog's alive." Merna's sitting again, her arms crossed. We watch the dog, her short shivering gait. She's very near the zamboni, wide jaws wide open, little saliva-drips hanging loosely from her thin black lips.

"There's blood on your shirt," I say to Erik without looking at him.

"There is?" Erik pulls at the hem, inspects the shirt.

"Killer," Aaron says, laughing. "There's the evidence." Bill Murray lifting slowly a bloody rag with his pen, placing the rag in a pneumatic tube.

"Killer," I repeat. "Killer, killer." The dog's on the ice. Sliding. "Slide," I say. Don't say thoughts, I think, emphatically. Merna's hand's touching Merna's face. The zamboni's circling vector-like. I feel a thick pain in my chest and stomach. I know I should watch my stomach, study it, videotape it somehow, but I ignore my stomach. I watch the dog, the zamboni. In my head the vectors are slowly aligning. I'm thinking about Merna and the little black dog and Merna's stomach which is flat and smooth and Merna's husband Noah who loves dogs and kittens and all living things and who'd be terribly disappointed, disgusted with me now, who, with his obscenely jointed fingers, would point me out to the sad rumpled detectives and wag his jointed index finger as the sad rumpled detectives dragged my un-struggling body away.

"What the?" says Erik.

"I'm," says Aaron.

I touch the wide glass partition and it's hard and smooth and cold. There's a dog-like sound, but pitched higher in a swelling way and echoing cavernously, and the dog's spinning sideways and the zamboni's moving inexorably in its inexorable vector and there's blood and shrieking, and the dog, now three-legged and bleedingly panicked, is still, except for a thin rapid shivering, its dog-body pressed against the white half-wall, the ice awash in thick black blood, the fourth leg loose and spinning somewhere, mid-ice.

TWENTY-FIVE

Merna's in the backseat with Aaron and the dog's wrapped in my coat in Merna's lap. Erik's slumped in the front-passenger seat. I'm driving.

"Fuck," Erik says. "Where the fuck are we fucking going?"

Aaron stares out the window.

"Where do you fucking go with a fucking three-legged fucking dog?"

"Calm down," Aaron says.

"Fuck."

"Panicking's useless, okay." Aaron looks down at the dog and smiles a thin-lipped smile. He rests his slim hand on the dog's little head. "We'll go to a veterinarian. That's what you do with dogs. Take them to veterinarians."

"It's practically fucking midnight. Where the fuck will we find a fucking veterinarian at fucking midnight?"

"At the veterinary hospital. Veteran. Veterinarian."

TWENTY-SIX

The security-guard body was very still. The eyes fluttered wildly. The little hairy head had collapsed on the broad uniformed shoulder and the wide flat mouth was wide open with the long pink tongue sort of rolled back and jammed into the teeth. The pudgy hands were strapped to the zamboni steering-wheel with white shoe-laces and beyond the shoe-laces the hands were very pale and white and the hand's wrinkles were very taut and pronounced in their paleness. Merna was on the ice, the dog in her arms. Aaron was laughing strangely, from a distance. Erik stared at the ice. I had stopped the zamboni. I was touching the uniformed shoulder which was rough and stained and wet. There was a patch and I touched the patch.

"It's bloody," Merna said. "It's an it."

"Look at this uniform," I said. "This uniform's very complicated, the stitching's complicated, I think, but why? I can't tell."

"I'm fucking sorry," Erik said. "I'm really fucking sorry."

Aaron was still laughing.

"It's bleeding. We should call Noah. Noah's not bleeding. Things shouldn't bleed."

"Who's Noah?" Aaron said.

I studied Aaron and Aaron was very fat, wide, his striped shirt stretched over his belly, and the belly was shaking, slim shoulders were shaking, everything was shaking so I touched the security-guard again and it moved.

"It's moving," I said.

"He," Erik said. "He's a fucking he."

TWENTY-SEVEN

"It's only a dog," Aaron says. "Dogs are only dogs. But they're survivors, if you're worried. I've seen three-legged dogs before, maybe five or six of them. A little imbalanced, but they heal and are happy, mostly. They run."

"I have the fucking leg," Erik says.

"What?" I say.

"I saw the fucking leg and fucking grabbed it. I thought someone might fucking need it to sew it the fuck back on for surgery or something."

"I don't think they can do that," I say.

Aaron leans toward the front-seats. "Let me see the leg," he says. Aaron puts his upturned hand between Erik and me. "I'll take care of it for you."

The little dog's whining in Merna's arms and Merna's weeping a little, quietly.

"Give me the leg."

Erik removes the leg from his pocket. It's a slim, jointed thing, very black and scabbed and wet. Slowly, waveringly, Erik places the leg in Aaron's upturned hand.

"Thank you."

"What do we do?" I ask.

Aaron rolls down his window and side-arms the leg into the snowy night-air. The leg's a flash of black beneath a streetlight, then gone. "That."

TWENTY-EIGHT

"It's moving," I said again. "Look at it," I said. "Somebody do something." The mouth opened and closed like an automated drawbridge and the tongue unfurled and wagged jerkily, as though disoriented or detached somehow, possessed of its own free-will. "Tongue," I said. Aaron's belly was shaking with laughter and the laughter was low and sad with a flat quality that filtered hollowly throughout the ice-skating arena. The security-guard cheek was sallow and cold. I touched it. The mouth continued to chomp drawbridge-like. The tongue and mouth formed slowly a word, almost muffled by Aaron's laughter, but there and solid and I was next to the word and with my ears I savored the word. The word was "It."

TWENTY-NINE

I direct the car along the snowy roads. There are dull streetlights and twinkle-y plastic reflectors. The car's moving smoothly and not sliding. A Shell station glowing in the distance, the pumps bright and clean beneath a high flat roof. There are no sounds except the low and limitless breathing of each person. The breaths are harsh and rasping and each person's a separate person, with lungs and heart and blood. I imagine my separate self with my own separate brain, and wonder what the separate me would think. I tell myself I'd only think what I'm thinking now because thought's a chemical process. If I were a separate me, I'd have the same chemicals. But I doubt myself and as the car's internal-combustion engine propels the car from streetlight to streetlight, I slowly think, that's wrong, stupid. My thoughts are random and undetermined because each being's a separate being and each thought's its own thought, motivation-less. "Unpredictable," I say.

"Emergency-room," Merna says. I don't hear her. I only see her thin pink lips.

"Huh?" I imagine the word emergency-room as a very long very straight highway that inclines slightly at a constant angle, and I can see very far beyond the horizon and beyond the horizon's this same road and in my rearview mirror the road disappears so there's no road and only a cloudy black nothing.

"Take it to the emergency room. Noah's there. Noah's working tonight. Noah will know what to do."

"Who's Noah?" Aaron asks.

"Is he a fucking veterinarian?" asks Erik. "Does he have an extra fucking leg?"

THIRTY

The security-guard eyes were shut. The mouth open and black. The nose porous, inflated. Within each nostril were thick black hairs that trembled with each inhalation. "It hurts," he said. "It hurts."

"Kill him already," Aaron said. "Where's your knife? He knows too much." Aaron's mouth rapidly chomped the air and when Aaron formed words each word was a short robotic thing. Constructing words slowly, the lungs compressing air, pushing it, each air molecule imbued with a direct and specific purpose. Aaron's hands convulsively closed into fists, his face expressionless. The fists were red and hairy, the knuckles round and white.

Merna quietly held the dog.

Erik shuddered and turned his back toward me. "I can't watch," he said. "I don't know what to look at. I don't know where to look."

I touched the porous security-guard nose.

"Blood on the ice," Aaron said. "Unsolved local mystery. The ice-kill-pades."

THIRTY-ONE

"What the hell happened?" Noah asks. Noah's stethoscope dangles from his wide hand. His eyes are very near the little dog's little black stump.

"Can you do something?" Merna asks.

Noah's obscenely jointed-fingers rattle together and caress the area around the little black stump and the little black stump trembles, vibrating rapidly, but Noah's fingers are persistent and investigative and calm. Noah's fingers are long and alien and I move away from the fingers and away from Aaron and Erik who stand together behind me and who are also alien and distant, either too wide or too narrow with limbs that are too long or that move in a slow and sudden way so that each moment I'm startled and fearful. Aaron and Erik's mouths move and there are words but I ignore the words and lay myself softly down on a narrow wooden bench and watch the white acoustic-tile ceiling and the gray fluorescent-light-panels and within each fluorescent-light-panel are three fluorescent-tubes, each lighted dully and flickering. "I don't have to move," I say. "I could lay here forever and no one would tell me I shouldn't."

Merna's there, standing above me. "He'll be okay," Merna says. "Noah's doing something." Merna sits near my head and touches my hair. "It was an accident."

"Accident," I say. "Tomorrow," I say.

"What?"

Aaron and Erik are distant and moving and I say to Merna, "Where are they going?"

"Back to the ice-rink, I guess. I don't know."

"I'm sleepy."

"You're coming tomorrow, aren't you?" Merna asks. Merna's hands are caressing her belly. I'm sleepy so I roll on my side and rest my arms cross-wise beneath my head which is heavy and warm and object-like. I suddenly imagine myself head-less and lightweight. I wonder if, head-less, with eyes in my shoulders or chest or something, I could move faster and more efficiently. Would I be outcast somehow? Stared at, mocked by small children, babies. Become then some kind of hermit, possessed of super-hero powers, but alone on a mountaintop, forever constructing tiny parking-lots. "You have to come, tomorrow, okay," Merna says. "I don't want to be the only one."

"What time is it?"

"Midnight."

"It is tomorrow," I say.

TOMORROW

THIRTY-TWO

I was eight. A car had hit the raccoon, bisected it. The little raccoon-legs still shivered and pulled forwardly as though, through raccoon-persistence, it could drag its bleeding half-body to the field beyond the road. I thought I should hurry home, half-raccoon slung over my shoulder, place it in Mother's hands or Merna's—hand it to Grandfather maybe, beg him to repair the raccoon, to reassemble it with superglue, rivets, a rivet gun, to get the power-drill from the garage, to drill clean holes through which we could reconnect the raccoon with rope or string, steel wire, something, to sew the raccoon-pieces into one perfect whole, maybe, to resurrect it. I poked the half-raccoon with a stick, flipped it, inspected its fleshy holes and jagged misshapen bones, its little pink muscle-tears and everywhere the thick black blood. I understood that death was normal, boring, particularly for raccoons, and imagined my body bisected, just as the raccoon was, little arms twitching forwardly, a girl in a pink corduroy jumper slowly poking me with a stick, transfixed as a half-lung oozed from my open abdomen. I heard a little gasp. It was Anastasia and Anastasia was small with long brown pigtails, her white crepe dress crinkled near the sleeves and around the lacy hem. Anastasia's mouth was open, her eyes little black dots. "I found it," I said. "It's our new pet." I poked the half-raccoon again. "Come look. It's a mutant-raccoon. Look at its funny waving legs. Look here, what should we name her?" Anastasia stood next to me, hands clasped before her. "We should operate," I said. "We'll call it Flossy, make an experiment. Play with the raccoon-muscles and the lungs and heart and stuff. Remove the lungs, collect lungs, petrify them, put them in formaldehyde, keep lungs, and livers maybe, hearts, petrified in jars on your bookshelf. You'd like that, wouldn't you? The formaldehyde-smell. We could make our own shelves for them. We could eat them. Or take the lungs, sew them together. An experiment, so we can discover things about lungs. We could take your lungs, okay. Make a lung-wall. We'll get a thousand lungs. Lung-tents, right? We'll get them at school."

"I don't want to experiment. Why'd you hurt that raccoon?"

The little raccoon-mouth opened and the raccoon-teeth were wet and slimy and thick with blood and the raccoon-jaws were shifted a little so that the raccoon-face was symmetry-less and swelled and the raccoon-eyes were bulging and misshapen and I wondered if I was hit by a car, would I be a half-me with a symmetry-less face and bulging misshapen eyes and would I try to pull my little half-body into a cold wet field? I quietly repeated my thoughts to Anastasia but she ignored them and focused her little black eyes on my throat and I watched the eyes as they wobbled there. We could've traded eyes. This is something I've considered many times. I could have Anastasia-eyes and Anastasia could have raccoon-eyes, or we could forego eyes and be eyeless in the field beyond the road. I wanted then to always be in the field beyond the road, with the raccoon, lying on the wet ground. A half-me hugging a half-raccoon. "It's my experiment," I said. "I'm investigating how raccoons survive with half-bodies and stuff so I can do magic-tricks and cut you in half with a chainsaw, so I can be a doctor. I could cut you in half and keep the bottom-half in the closet, the top-half in my bedroom in a big fish-tank or on my nightstand attached to a plaque."

"I don't want to be cut in half and die."

"Everything has to die. Besides that's why I'm doing the experiment. So you won't die right away, see, and I'd probably save you when I'm a doctor. Glue your half-bodies together."

"I don't want to."

"I'd put you back together. Little thread and glue. Gluestick," I said. "Gluestick," I said again. Anastasia didn't answer. "What about the raccoon?" I asked. "Look at all the blood. It's going to die probably. I should kill it now, shouldn't I? We should kill it dead?"

"I'd probably bleed until I die and then I'd be dead so don't cut me in half—you can't, it's weird and mean, I'll tell Grandpa." Anastasia moved a little and watched the ground. "I'll get you and shoot you probably. I'll stop you."

"Forget it. We have to experiment on this raccoon before it's gone. We need to get some knives or something, some rope."

"You don't have to." Anastasia was almost crying. "You could fix it or Grandpa could and someone could fix it so don't kill it just fix it please."

"Grow up," I said. "It's going to raccoon-heaven with the other raccoons and they probably climb in little heaven-trees and fight and stuff or maybe they just go and burn up forever."

"I hate you," Anastasia said. "You're mean and nasty." Anastasia was running as she said this. "I'm telling Grandpa," she said.

"Go be a liar," I said. "You're the nasty liar." The raccoon was still moving but I left it on the road and walked into the field which was wet and cold with tall grass and thick mud and the mud was slippery and dark and brown and my feet seemed to disappear beneath the mud only to reappear a step later, and the mud was in my shoes and soaking my socks and I moved my wet little toes, thought about toes, how my toes were wet and moving, how my shoes held carefully the wet, moving toes. I imagined myself buried in mud, moving my toes beneath the mud, sleeping quietly in the muddy field, then waking later with mud-toes and a mud-body and a pet mud-raccoon, or beyond that somehow, waking on a beach at night near a rowboat full of mud and wet sand and sitting with the oars, wet from the waves, half my body here, half my body there.

THIRTY-THREE

"Will it live?" I hear Merna ask.

"Probably," Noah's saying. "Stitched her up, a little morphine. Sleeping now. I'll determine what must be done, later. I may have to put her down. She's in a lot of pain and I can't establish any definitive cause, not for certain. Her musculature, internal organs, other things, could've been damaged when the leg was torn."

My neck's sore and pinched so I sit up and stretch. The room's white and empty except for Noah and Merna who are standing near the low front-counter. Behind Noah and Merna are gray flat-screen monitors, screensavers running—space travel, bouncing balls. There are wide bulky desks with plain melamine tops and behind them, six metal clipboards hanging in a row. Noah's very tall and thin and his arms and legs are long and thin, delicate. Noah's wearing thin square glasses which reflect the fluorescent-lights in pale bands and obscure his round black eyes.

"How is she?" Noah asks. He points his obscenely jointed index finger at me.

"I'm okay," I say.

"She's just tired," Merna says.

"I said I'm okay."

"We'll get coffee or something. Take her home maybe. Put her to bed. She'll be fine. Call me, okay? About the dog."

"Of course."

"I said I'm perfectly fine," I say.

Noah hugs Merna. "I have to check on my patients," he says. With his obscenely jointed fingers, Noah squeezes my shoulder, then smiles a fatless smile, his teeth wet, glistening with saliva. I want to remove them, to remove one tooth, to hold it there, wet in the fluorescent-light. I think about saliva, acids, mouths, digestion. About dentists, New Mexico. If the New Mexico desert performs some kind of digestion. Owls perched on gigantic teeth. Sharp, in a row. Who would monitor them? The Carlsbad Caverns, swallowing people, families. Some kind of giant robot, controlled by Bill Murray.

Merna's standing in front of me. "Ready?"

"I'm ready." We step outside. It's icy and the parking-lot's wide and empty except for an ambulance and Merna's car. "Why does Noah hate me?"

"What are you talking about?"

"I know the whole deal," I say. I sit in the passenger-seat. "How he glares at me, how he moves when he's near me, kind of tentative, quick and violent, maybe, like he's holding a butterfly-knife, thrusting the butterfly-knife slowly into my face, like he's choosing where to thrust the knife, my eye-socket maybe, you know, to get the least resistance, to kill quickly, quietly. He'd choose my left eye probably, then slide the knife in, pop an eye out, maybe two, doctor-like, you know, precisely, cut out little brain-chunks. Bowls of brain-chunks." I knead my temples with flat palms. "Probably imagines how to dissect me, how to dispose of my dissected body, my organs, fingers, lungs, where to dump me, in a canvas sack off the Golden Gate Bridge or in a dirty restaurant dumpster, maybe, next to fish-guts, gristle." I imagine my body in one-thousand pieces piled carefully in a canvas sack, abandoned behind a McDonald's in New Mexico, the American flag draped over it. My body rotting, but nobody to move the flag, to see the pieces beneath the flag. Or a child, led by the stench, slowly pulling the flag, now wet, molded, away from the fleshy remainders. "I wonder if he tells you about the fish-guts and gristle, or he probably thinks you'd discover his little hobby, that you'd call the police, so it's like his secret hobby and when you're sixty or something you go into his study and find the newspaper clippings, little bone trophies maybe, trachea pieces, kneecaps, clavicles strung together into necklaces. Like pookah shells maybe. I don't know."

Merna doesn't say anything for a while. The streetlights stretch across our faces. "Want to get coffee?" she asks. "Or go home and sleep or something? It's very late." She yawns.

"I'm getting too close to this Noah thing aren't I? Is it scary?"

"Quit it, okay."

"Sorry."

"We're making a family."

"I said I was sorry."

"You always say that. Who cares if you're sorry? What's sorry? You're always so negative, so crazily paranoid—I can't ever tell when you're joking. What if you're not joking and somehow Noah has this butterfly-knife, a hundred of them, then I wouldn't want our twins near these butterfly-knives. I don't like to think about things like that. About knife-blades You put these ideas in my head, and then I have to forget them. Just act normally. Be like Growing Pains or something. Be a little Roseanne."

I don't answer. Merna's shaking her head and Merna's thin pink lips are moving quickly and soundlessly. I watch the digital-clock in the dashboard which is composed of tiny red-lighted bars and think about how these red-lighted bars shuffle and reshuffle, horrifically, so you can never tell which bar is which. I cover my mouth and yawn. My cell-phone ring-tone plays a little song. "Good morning," I say into my cell-phone.

"It's done," Erik says.

"Oh good," I answer. "What's done?"

"The security-guard."

"Huh?" I think about done and the significance of the end of one thing, the beginning of another.

"What's next?"

"Coffee," I say. "What does done mean?"

"The usual place?"

"Done?" I say.

"Okay." Erik turns off his cell-phone.

"They're done," I say to Merna. "Coffee, I guess." Merna's lips continue to move soundlessly in a sudden and jerky way. I watch them closely, their pinkness, the stuttering shuffled way each lip pulls from the other then clamps back into place, the wet tongue darting between the lips and retreating behind the wet teeth, waiting for the next daredevil move, springing crazily outward. "Done's not always the final word, I think. Could mean anything probably, and Erik probably meant that he melted all the ice, drained it into a tanker-truck, shipped the tanker-trunk to Lisbon." I pause. Who would drive the tanker-truck? Who would back it onto the ship? And drive the ship? What flags would it fly? Could we sell them for a profit? "For the children," I say. "For the children who, before this melted ice-water comes, were swimming through dirty alleys and with long thin tongues were licking little dewdrops from cold trash-dumpsters probably, from the dumpster-bottoms, their mouths coated with rust. Maybe Erik drained the ice-water into a million baby-bottles and held the baby-bottles to the mouths of the children who suckled at them." Merna turns the car onto a wide empty highway. Streetlights flash through the windows regularly, strobe-like. "Right?" I ask. "It could be something like that."

"No." Merna says. Then, after a moment, "No."

THIRTY-FOUR

I photographed Merna's prom-queen dress, hanging narrowly from her thin shoulders as she slouched next to her prom-king in our family-room. He was tall and thick and hairy and wore a white tuxedo-jacket with creased black slacks and a black bow-tie, shiny black oxfords peeking out beneath the creased slacks. His name was Anthony. I over-exposed the film so that everywhere a white light suffused their bodies, but made fifty eight-by-tens anyway, hung them in every room, handed the others out at school. "That picture's disgusting, I hate you," Merna said. "Bitch," she was muttering. She didn't like photography. We were walking home from school, wide backpacks slung over our shoulders, and it was sunny and cool and wind moved along the tree-branches. It was May.

"I captured a moment in prom-history."

"We look like poltergeists or something. We look like holograms."

"Artistic expression and stuff. I wanted to show the 'innate ephemerality of the human-body as object.'"

"Whatever."

"I call it, Prom-Queen Alley. I think that's a good title."

"It's a shitty title," Merna said. "I think you should call it, Bitch Photographer as Bitch-Slut.'"

"I like that. I like naming things. I think I'll call you Cross-patch. My new creation."

"What's that supposed to mean?"

"I don't know. I read it somewhere once." We were walking along a narrow two-lane road. Along the curb were dozens of gray sedans, each sedan slightly different from every other sedan, but only in small ways, so that from a distance they seemed clones. Up close there were chrome tailpipes or bumper-stickers, neoprene steering-wheel covers, baby-on-board window-shades. I imagined cloned cars, cloned people, marching, dentists in New Mexico shoulder to shoulder, clogging Main Street, each one wrapped in an American flag. Lisbon. A car factory there. Grandfather holding a pneumatic drill. "Everything's the same," I said.

"What?"

"Everything's different."

There was a driveway and a gray sedan, hood up. Behind the hood was a shirtless boy with little black chest-hairs and cavernous black eyes. The boy slammed the hood shut and moved carefully toward Merna and me.

"What's up Merna?" the boy said. "Who's this?"

"I'm me."

"It talks," the boy said. The boy laughed quietly. "Kind of."

"My sister," Merna said. "She's mine."

"Oh?" The boy scanned my body with his cavernous black eyes. "Doesn't look much like you."

"I'm the 'innate ephemerality of the human-body as object.'"

"Whatever," the boy said. "Check out my rims. I just got these rims.

Spinners, they sort of spin backwards when I'm driving. Fucking tight. I'm telling you."

Merna squatted and inspected the rims and the boy leaned and looked down Merna's blouse. "Got them today?" she asked.

"The rims are very shiny," I said. "They sparkle."

"Pretty awesome," Merna said.

"Spinners spin?" I asked. "Sparkle, sparkle." I was laughing a little.

The boy glared at me. "Yeah, they spin." He squatted next to Merna. "What's wrong with your sister? Is she a retard or something?"

"Oh, stop it." Merna was giggling.

"Just wondering, cause, I mean, look at her eyes which are kind of weird and shaky, kind of cloudy, you know, and maybe she has down-syndrome or something. You know down-syndrome? Corky? I don't want to hurt her feelings, if she has any, I mean if she can think or whatever. I heard down-syndrome kids don't have feelings cause they can't remember more than five seconds at time. Is that true?" The boy was whispering hoarsely. "You keep her in a cage, feed her dog-food or something? In her own bowl." He paused, wagging his finger. "She should have her own bowl, you know. It's more humane that way." He pointed his chin toward me and sniffed loudly. "How often do you change her diapers?"

Merna giggled a little and nervously looked at me.

I didn't say anything.

"You want a ride," the boy asked Merna. He stood and leaned against his sedan. "Your backpack's tight. I like that zipper-pocket in back. Where'd you get it? Were there other colors?"

"I'm going home," I said.

"Can she find her way home alone?" the boy whispered. "She looks confused."

I shook my head. "Bye," I said. I moved along the sidewalk.

"Wait," Merna said.

"Just a little drive," the boy said. "We'll go to the mall. I need a hat, and a new backpack. Would you help me choose a hat?"

I watched Merna and the boy over my shoulder as I walked away.

"Now that this bitch's gone," the boy said loudly, "you want to go for a ride?" He was giggling. "We can drive right over her if you want."

I walked faster.

"Fuck off okay," Merna said. Merna was next to me, her hand on my shoulder. The hand was small and wrinkled and warm. The fingernails were purple and very smooth and my stride and Merna's stride were the same stride for a while. "I'm sorry," Merna said. "I'm really sorry." Merna's eyes were tight, squinting in slits and I made my eyes squint in exactly the same way, eyelashes at the same angle, one solid furrow centered on my forehead. Our backpacks brushed against our backpacks and the matching sleeves of our white blouses slid together and apart. It was warm and the houses along the road spread out until there was so much open space you could see the horizon-line in the distance, curving away. For a moment, you could imagine lying in the grass, backpacks as pillows, waiting for someone to say anything, for an airplane to New Mexico to wing by, its propellers whirring invisibly, for a Cadillac to roll to a stop, power-windows descending full speed, the humming behind them, your own mouth humming, and the smell then of May.

THIRTY-FIVE

"I worked in the Portuguese tin-can factory," Grandfather said. "After the war. That's where I met your grandmother. We danced between the tin-cans, gigantic pyramids of them, a waltz or something. The can-can." I was fourteen. It was July and humid. Outside the lawn was patchy and brown, the blades flat and limp between wide beds of cracked mud. I sat on a tall silver stool, turning side to side. Grandfather stood near the stove, red-silicone potholders encasing his hands, eyes fixed on the oven-timer, motionless, brows furrowed crazily so that I wanted to hold them, to reach out with my tiny hands, fit my fingers between wrinkles, beneath the eyeball itself, holding the skull. I spun on my stool and watched my tiny feet, my thin little toes and toenails. Grandfather continued, "We produced thirty-two styles in twelve sizes and really these cans were for beans and pineapples and paint and oil, and we made some for peas and olives, condensed milk, other things. Snakes. You sweated forever like hell. One-hundred-fifty degrees in the factory, everyone completely naked except for a company-issued loin-cloth, and always two glasses of water from a riot. Know what the secret was?"

I shook my head.

"Drugged water. Pacify angry populations. Really, it's the easiest way, you know, like fluoridation. Government research has proven this over and over. Drugs. Seriously. Fluoride. Think about it." Grandfather hummed a little. "Drugs," he said again.

"Oh? Hmm."

"What are we really talking about?"

"I don't know."

Grandfather was baking blueberry pies in tiny foil pie-trays. Thirty or forty of them already, covering every counter, the tabletop, filling cabinets, refrigerator shelves. Pies in drawers, in the kitchen sink, on the floor. I could smell the warmth, the sugar, browned pie-crusts, the sulfurous cooling of foil.

"Blueberry pies and drugs?" I asked. "Like pie-drugs."

"Pie was invented by a Roman or something, Cato the Elder. Write that down." Grandfather was laughing. "Cato found that the best way to pacify Roman populations was to drug them with pies. His pie was more of a tart with honey and goat-cheese, probably—there are several surviving recipes, but who's to say which is the right one—anyway, he added, I don't know, hemlock or something, strychnine, tricked the would-be rioters, the probable evil-doers, into eating these pie-tart-things with hemlock, had to be hemlock because that was how Romans liked to poison people, and every day Cato'd send out a cart for the dead, poisoned, would-be rioters, and sometimes two carts, horse-drawn carts, or donkeys maybe, and he'd have his men gather the bodies and dump them in the river, or if the weather was inclement, pile them up and burn them, in a big pyre, ridding Rome of evil-doers and simultaneously warming nearby homes. He was very innovative."

"Are you drugging these pies so you can burn probable evil-doers too?"

"What pies?"

"These blueberry pies," I said. I pointed at the blueberry pies. "What are all these pies for?"

"Oh, these pies. These pies are bribes," Grandfather said. "Bartering. Pie's a valuable commodity now and I'll trade it for other valuable commodities on the commodity-market, you know, like diamonds or something, rocket-launchers."

"I want a pie, can I have one? They look sweet and I'd like to eat one or maybe just a piece, maybe if there's sort of an ugly one or one that doesn't seem whole and perfect or as valuable. Or maybe you could make a special pie for me and Merna or something, you know family-like, a special blueberry pie. You could make a special blueberry pie I think, it could just be a normal pie but special because it's for me and Merna and Mom, maybe."

Grandfather opened the oven and removed a blueberry pie and stood very still and watched the kitchen-counters, the blueberry pie in his hands.

"Mom would like a blueberry pie. We could share them you know, slices of the pie, for Mom and me and Merna."

Grandfather's eyes seemed very distant and concentrated. The grandfather-eyes were immovable, locked into place, bolted eyes, attached to a mountain-face. Mountain-climbers would pass the eyes maybe, use them to mark their trail, or camp there, baking blueberry pies in miniature pie-tins and offering tiny pie-slivers to the eyes as though to a dismembered Santa Claus.

"You don't have to though," I said. "I mean we don't need a blueberry pie and really a special blueberry pie like that's probably narcissistic or something and it was a stupid idea. Don't worry, I realize it was a dumb idea and I won't tell Mom about the blueberry pies or anything." I stopped for a moment and tried to forget the eyes. "And I won't even ask for another thing like that again. I won't ask for anything. I didn't mean to go around demanding blueberry pies which would be terribly frivolous and stuff and people should probably work for their blueberry pies because it's a valuable commodity and I can probably make my own pies and maybe I'll make you an apple pie sometime, if you like apples which I don't really know because I never asked you about that."

Grandfather turned the oven-knob to OFF and set the blueberry pie on an empty stovetop burner. "It's okay," he said. "Pie? It's really okay." Grandfather shook his head slowly. "There's enough pie now." He stepped slowly out of the kitchen with little shuffling old-man steps, his tiny black eyes half-closed, and I followed him and we were in the family-room together near the sofa which was empty, plastic-covered, apathetic, the end of all couches.

"Yeah it's okay," I said. "I mean pies are unhealthy, sort of insidious, probably addicting somehow, the sugar, the crystals of it bonding together, in your stomach. I don't know anything. And I didn't really want one anyway because it would make me spoiled probably and fat and ugly and useless. I would have a distended belly and lay on the couch groaning if I ate it. If I ate them. And I wouldn't stop. I'd eat all the pies. I'd roll in them. I'd lob them out windows at passing Cadillacs. And blueberry pies are commodities, not for eating, I mean I don't want any pie. I was only joking about having one. Nobody should eat these pies," I said. "They should be preserved. They should be locked up. We should think of some way to keep these pies safe."

THIRTY-SIX

"Blueberries," I say aloud.

"Hmm," Merna says.

"Pie." The car console's lighted, running off the battery. Denny's is warm-looking. Through the windows are customers with large round heads, wide oval mouths, the wide mouths open, moving excitedly, and there's pancakes, hash-browns, coffee, salt shakers, single-serving jellies, trayfuls. I can imagine holding the jellies, pyramiding them. The windows are steamed and through them the mouths blur and I think about heat and oxygen, about all mouths as one mouth, lying quietly in a parking-lot, in a pile. Which mouth would speak? All of them at once? "Should we go inside and wait? Get a table?"

"No," Merna says. "I like it here. I like it in my car. It has comfortable seats. Paid extra so I need to use them, you know. That's what Noah says. 'Use your damn seats,' he says." Merna leans back. "Seat-warmers," she says. She pushes a button. "Feel the seat-warmer. We can listen to the radio, I like the radio, just to listen to it. Doesn't matter what it is. Do you want to listen to something? Just these voices you know. Somebody talking somewhere. Who cares what they're saying?" Merna removes a mirror from her purse, opens it, examines her face from several angles. She focuses the mirror on her eyes and eyebrows and with a little round pad Merna smoothes her eyebrows. "How are you feeling?"

"What do you mean? I'm fine. I'm pretty happy. It was my birthday."

"Happy birthday?"

"Exactly."

"On birthdays I always feel closer to death," Merna says. "Wrinkled, you know, at the end, but I'm only a little older than you. You've been strange, a little distant. Grandpa said something, and Grandma. Like something's bothering you, you know, like when you're talking, there's this pause, as though you're translating or something, as though you're conferring with someone. It's like satellite-telephone or something. Like you're in Afghanistan."

"I'm a little tired," I say. "Allergies. Black mold in my bathroom, on the ceiling, behind the toilet, and it took a week to get the maintenance-man to remove it—I'd already inhaled the spores, when I went to the bathroom probably, when I was sleeping, so the spores are in my lungs, stuck there, clogging them, killing lung-cells, breeding, which makes me tired because my body has to produce more white blood-cells to fight the black mold, the black mold colonies, the societies of them, those cells, to keep me from dying and also because the mold's inhibiting my lungs somehow so my oxygen intake's smaller, weaker, my lungs oxygen-less, or oxygen-starved kind of, weak, slowly gasping, you know, for air."

Merna nods quietly as she watches cars pass along the highway, the tiny mirror still nestled in her palm.

"Grandpa should be worried about you Merna, not me. You're pregnant with twins, married to Noah with his weird hands. You'll have to raise the twins alone. Noah works like a hundred hours a week, sleeps at the hospital, on a gurney, right? You'll be always alone and talk only to the babies, babies who can only cry or burp, so you end up walking dark alleys in nightgowns, banging your head against dumpsters—probably the twins'll be boys and the twin boys'll grow up without a paternal influence which will make them violent, dangerous, apt to take risks, knife-fights, baseball-bats, drag-races, chicken at night with no headlights, drugs and alcohol, and you can't stop that because teenage boys only care about exerting themselves on the universe, existence and stuff—also negating the universe, fear of death or something and they'll ask you where Noah is and you'll tell the twins he's at work saving people in the emergency-room, which will internalize their anger somehow, make them quiet and passive, angry at those saved people, searching them out, in their casts, on their gurneys, looking savagely for oxygen-tanks to switch off, IVs to cut."

"Noah doesn't work that much."

"He only exists at work. He only exists in his emergency-room."

"He gets vacations."

"Emergency-room," I say. "Anyway, if there's an emergency, which could happen on vacation or any time really, moment to moment, at every moment, like he's potentially talking to the twins, teaching them important life skills, speech, cooking, street-crossing, his long fingers grasping carefully their tiny shoulders, and there's the cell-phone, the hospital, a surgery. The boys never learn to speak. At street corners they panic, scream silently. You lock them in basements, feed them scraps, orange-rinds. The police come and absorb them."

"Don't worry, Noah and I'll be fine, the babies are fine."

"They're not even babies yet."

We don't talk for a while. Aaron's Lexus parks near the end of the Denny's parking-lot. Aaron and Erik stroll slowly into the Denny's, feet dragging through the ice and snow. They're laughing, their heads bobbing side to side.

"Why do you fuck with Grandma?" Merna says.

"Shouldn't we go inside?"

"She's a good person and she loves you, I mean, you don't know how much she cares, how you can hurt her so easily. Like, you know, she made you that dinner, a pie, keeps your room pristine, unchanged, stuck in time."

I open the car-door. "There's Aaron and Erik."

"Basically our mother maybe and she loves you. Just wants you to be a little normal, sometimes, a person. You could drop by for dinner, or take her to breakfast. We go out to breakfast every Sunday, you know. You could come for once. We've all invited you."

We step in and out of long streetlight parallelograms and my shadow's long and indistinct. "Coffee probably. Coffee and fries maybe, blueberry pie." I have the sudden sense that Grandfather's baking pies at Denny's, covering slowly every countertop, every table, monopolizing ovens, burners, the refrigerator.

Merna's walking next to me. "You could have a worse Grandma. She could have hammers, pliers, could torture you, dump you in gasoline or something. She could stomp you, you know. And she probably should, or should've, maybe then, when you were a kid? I should've. Sometimes I just want to tie you up. She could've burned you with matches, candles, lighters. She could've punched you with an iron. Kicked you down the stairs or something. She did none of these things."

"Thanks Merna," I say.

"Tell her about work. Are you in school? We don't know anything about you. Be a person. Send an email. A card, with pictures. Anything."

"What do you mean? 'Be a person?' What could you possibly mean? I'm not a person? What am I?"

"You're my sister and I'm your sister so we're sisters and we have to be honest because nothing else in the world can be honest with anything except for us two sisters." Merna points her eyes. "We're the only ones who can understand each other, who speak the same language, somehow, so it's us, here. You can be us, you can. Okay. For Grandma, Grandpa. You can, can for us."

"Oh," I say. We sit. Menus hide Aaron and Erik's faces.

"It's good. You're a good person," Merna says. "You can be a person."

"I'm at Denny's," I say.

THIRTY-SEVEN

I've never been to New Mexico. I know this objectively. There are no pictures, memories. There's an image of a parking-lot, a minivan. Could be anywhere. Grandfather may have taken me many places but I see his face always in a Cadillac. I see a window opening, a window closing.

Merna was small when she towed me behind her bicycle, when we moved from one sidewalk to another, until finally the shopping-mall loomed before us, bright and dark, flat everywhere, center-perfect in the parking-lot. Flanked by a thousand gray and motionless cars. Minivans angled precisely in their slots. Where was Anastasia? Was she too small? Merna told me it was here we could find the things we wanted. "We could be anyone," she might have said. "We could be anywhere."

Walking along the tiles, carefully avoiding the spaces between them, we were anyone. We were anywhere. I know this objectively.

There were thousands of people walking and we moved between them.

There were no people.

It was empty and Merna stood next to me, searching the parking-lot for Cadillacs. There were wide blankets upon which lay a thousand flags, all folded into neat triangles, small cards with prices before them.

Billowing tents behind. I imagined living in the tents, moving the tents from one parking-lot to another. If all parking-lots were the same parking-lot. How much for a ticket to Lisbon? Merna didn't know. Could a parking-lot lead us there?

THIRTY-EIGHT

The table's a smooth brown rectangle, wood grain beneath lacquer, the grain printed on paper. The edge's lined with a cold metal-strip. I place my forearm against the strip, feel the metal until my arm feels cold and metallic. I imagine wood grain flags, split trees. One-million rings sewed into thin white cloth. Tied tightly to the metal strips. Erik laying the flags flat in New Mexico, at the Wal-Mart parking-lot. Handwritten cardboard signs. Six dollars. Six-thousand. Merna, Bill Murray at her side, knives in hand. A flag bigger than the parking-lot, a thousand faces sewed into it, flapping there, above our tents. Merna's shadow over my face. Where's Grandfather?

"Aluminum," I say.

Erik yawns.

Aaron's eyes are small and watery and red. "I'm tired," Aaron says. "Could sleep under this table. Shut off lights, bed down and sleep, dried gum, cockroaches maybe. Toast-crumbs. Scrambled eggs. Whatever. Through the breakfast rush."

"Yeah," Erik says, his eyes flat and handless. "Sure."

Merna stands. "Be back."

"Where's she going?" Aaron says. "I'm deaf and alone."

"I'm sleepy," I say. "I'm sleepy, sleepy."

"You could sleep over at my place," Erik says. "I'd even let you have the bed."

"It's my apartment," I say. "My bed. I made it."

"No, not beds at all, no beds—sleepy lungs." Aaron leans against the window, his thin face suddenly wide and fat, flushed. "Breathless, happiest lungs ever. Heart's napping. I'm pale. See. Pale." Aaron holds his hand to Erik's face. "Out of blood. Okay. Bored of blood. New blood, special parasite blood. Is that right? Parasites, right?"

"Sure, maybe," Erik says.

"Noah gave her morphine," I say.

"Who's Noah?" Erik asks.

"Noah's sleepy too," Aaron says. "Sleepless doctors who nap only on empty gurneys, always ready to wake, dreaming lightly, not restful. Correct though, I think. Sleep's a waste."

I make a tower from grape and marmalade single-serving jelly-containers. "Security is security," I say. I shove the tower aside and watch it wobble, then crumble container by container. I restack them. I build out. I get more jellies from the next table.

Aaron crosses his long thin arms over his wide round belly. "Never so tired before. Hurts to yawn, jaw's don't open that way. Have to work, conference-call, to be lethargic, slow-witted, fired, homeless, no credit cards. Sleeping in dumpsters. Should be beds everywhere. Communist beds. Sleeping-rooms with wide queen-sized beds and soft down-comforters, nine pillows."

"No sleeping." Erik's little fist knocks down my tower. "Wrecking crew," he says, laughing weakly.

"Real live ducks," Aaron says. "Warm feathery ducks, amputated legs, wings, beakless, headless, you know, living warmth. Maybe food-bearing tubes built into the bed, introduced intravenously to the ducks. Sleep in a duck-pile."

I begin the reconstruction of my tower.

"Fuck ducks, whatever," Erik says.

Aaron's laughing mouth opens and closes rapidly, each laugh accompanied by a solid, vicious bite, and it seems, suddenly, that Aaron menaces the air, monopolizes it, siphoning all oxygen into twin oxygen-tanks, transforming his lungs, his body, into a vacuum. Our lungs may collapse. Erik slumping. Merna returning from the restroom, hands on her throat. The waitress dropping then a tray of drinks. All of us, Merna, the waitress, me, lying there on the floor. Motionless. Cheeks sucked in. A melting ice-cube.

"Careful," I whisper. "The air."

Erik stares blankly.

"Nevermind."

Aaron's laughing. "Put everyone to sleep. Naptime everyone. Everyone take a nap. Dictator declares naptime. First act. The nap-act."

"Time to piss," Erik says. He disappears.

Merna slides in next to me.

"Naptime?" Aaron asks. "Naps?"

"Can't sleep here. Can't."

"Nap-act?"

"You might suffocate me, with a pillow, or sweater. Plastic shopping-bag over my face, the bag tightened until I only breathe plastic, until my lungs are plastic. I could be plastic. You could turn me into plastic somehow. Remolding. The right temperature. Make me into a table. Into a parasol."

"Never suffocate pretty girls. Against my personal philosophy."

"That's what I said."

"Dog's okay?"

"Yeah."

"Good. Won't suffocate dog today."

Our coffees arrive. I drink.

"Security-guard?" Aaron says.

I'm watching our reflections in the window.

"Is a security-guard." Aaron says.

Erik returns. My tower towers. Aaron laughs quietly. Erik in his seat.

"Don't worry," Aaron says. "Only talked, only had a little chat."

"I bet," I say. "We should call the police."

"Paid him," Erik says. "Not police. Money."

"Where's your phone Merna? Where's mine? Police's a good solution."

"Only gave him money. Everyone wants or needs money," Aaron says.

"Yeah, money," Erik says.

"After the ass-kicking."

"Police'll help," I say to Merna. "They'll have notepads, flashlights."

"Oh?" Erik says.

"Batons. They can write things."

"Money and ass-kicking's the winning negotiation technique," Aaron says. "He's happy. Satisfied. Asked him, this was before I kicked his little face, and he said he was very satisfied and that he was going to take a nap. See, nap-act. Mandated naps. Siestas. Nap-revolution. Are you tired? Like you haven't slept in days. Maybe never slept. Don't know about sleep?"

"Wasn't much blood," Erik says. "Thought there'd be more blood."

Our food arrives in steaming baskets lined carefully with wax-paper.

"Hungry," Aaron says. "Really hungry." Aaron stuffs french fries into Aaron's mouth and slowly, mechanically, chews, and while Aaron chews mechanically, Aaron grunts softly, burps, and Aaron's little eyes close. "Good food," Aaron says. "Good," he says, his eyes still closed.

"No ass-kicking," Erik says. "Never any such thing."

"Fuck," Aaron says, chomping through french fries, waving other french fries toward Erik. "There's always ass-kicking."

I feel distracted and tired and my coffee's warm and bitter so I hold the coffee in my mouth, imagine the security-guard sitting at our table, ordering coffee, blueberry pie. When the security-guard says, "Blueberry pie," the waitress slaps him. She says, "I'll remove your brain," which make no sense. I understand objectively that the security-guard's normal, man-like, large with warm sleepy eyes, thin white hairs, that he moves powerfully forward, sideways, crab-like at angles, with firm steps, firm feet. That he firmly demands blueberry pie, firmly chews the pie until there's no pie. That he's always uniformed, that he speaks little, if ever, but communicates directly with eyes, hands. That waitresses become suddenly fearful and cold, that every nearby human moves incrementally away. I could have a remote-control for him, could move him when he needs to be moved. "Cocoon-terrorism," I say. "Caterpillar-death." I don't mean what I say. Nobody answers. "Let's be anarchists?" I say. There is fluorescent-light. There are windows. "Let's be fascists or something."

THIRTY-NINE

"You're my little anarchist," Grandfather said. "Know what that means?"

I shook my head. I was fifteen. It was September.

"Means you've got personality. You're clever. You know. Anarchist! Surprising word, has a little punch, gumption, probably. Something you tell police when you get pulled over for speeding. Stare into cop-eyes and say, 'I've got anarchism in my heart,' and the cop's surprised, a little scared, and you say, 'but not the way you think,' then smile your little smile and you'll never get a ticket. You've got anarchism, I think."

"I also have caterpillars," I said.

"Caterpillars are interesting too," Grandfather said. "Insects with hair. Cocoons. Metamorphose into big winged butterflies or moths or something and flitter around prettily. Humankind could learn something from caterpillars—I'm not sure what. Maybe something about embracing nature and I don't just mean plants and trees and stuff but maybe embrace instincts, things like that, building mud huts, farming, subjugating and dominating cows, goats, plants, or maybe how to design stylish clothing, windows. How to flitter."

We were at the zoo watching the penguins swim around.

"Penguins are good too. Very stylish. Life of the party."

"Penguin," I said.

"Are you hungry?"

"Can't eat penguins. Penguin-steaks are probably illegal or something," I said.

"Correct. No penguin eating. But there's ice cream around here somewhere."

"Ice cream?"

"With waffle-cones and strawberries and other things."

"I don't know," I said. "Ice cream's sort of evil, isn't it? Made from milk and sugar, but somehow unwholesome, like, isn't it evil to steal cows-milk from milk cows and to then change it, unnaturally, to filter in sugars and preservatives and berries and chocolate and waffles. It's a little like playing god."

"Milk cows make milk and wouldn't exist otherwise. You have to eat ice cream, drink milk, cheese, yogurt, otherwise those milk cows are redundant and pointless, would have to be slaughtered which would be disgusting and bloody, and might take years. A real revolution."

"We could save the cows, couldn't we? Together? We could invade cow-farms with semi-trucks and steal the cows, drive them to Alaska or Canada. Some place safe and unexpected. Belize?"

"It'd take a lifetime."

"Important work though. We'd design and build cow-saving submarines and transport the cows to uninhabited desert islands, recruit teenagers, college-students. It could be the 'bovine-underground.'"

"You draw up the plans. I'll get the ice cream."

"Okay."

"Ice cream's over there," Grandfather said. "See the umbrella. Be back shortly."

Grandfather walked toward the ice cream stand. I sat on a nearby bench. There was a slight breeze so I hugged my shoulders and thought about Grandfather's over-the-calf black and yellow argyle birthday-socks about which that morning Grandfather had said, "When I wear these with shorts I'm visible to drunk-drivers and spy-satellites." I touched my socks and watched Grandfather's socks and thought about how our socks were different socks though often my socks and Grandfather's socks intermingled in the washer and later in the dryer and that our socks shared static-electricity sometimes. Then, momentarily, I couldn't see Grandfather's over-the-calf black and yellow argyle birthday-socks so I stood and moved toward the umbrella, which was white and green, and concentrated on the umbrella and the little black ice cream bar stitched into the umbrella and I wanted suddenly to be beneath that umbrella so I moved quickly and recklessly toward it. My shoulder smashed an old woman in a rain-bonnet who said, "Excuse you, bitch." I nearly trampled a small girl in denim overalls. My hands moved in front of me, opening and closing as though my hands wanted to grab something. I didn't know what my hands wanted to grab.

I stood beneath the ice cream stand umbrella.

I remained very still.

I could see Grandfather's argyle socks.

"Here," Grandfather said. His hand was wrinkled and spotted and shaky. The hand held my ice cream.

I took my ice cream. "Thank you," I said. I held the ice cream and watched the ice cream and the ice cream didn't move. The ice cream didn't disappear.

FORTY

Merna and I walk to Merna's car and sit there. From the passenger-window, we can see Aaron and Erik pushing one another.

"I can touch anything," Erik yells. "Every fucking thing's mine."

Merna backs out of the parking space, her tires crunching slowly the snow.

"I'll eat your goddamn arm," Erik yells.

As we turn out onto the Interstate, Erik's fist cocks and punches Aaron's face. Aaron's hands reach and Aaron and Erik are clutching one another tightly. They topple slowly. The car rolls swiftly along and Aaron and Erik are distant and shadowy and invisible in the darkness and I imagine what Aaron and Erik must be thinking as they embrace there in the snow. I imagine their fingertips, the snow numbing them, clumps of hair between them, a security-guard standing over their wet bodies, arms crossed, each arm muscled, cord-like. Is the security-guard Bill Murray? No. There's a biplane. Merna could fly the biplane. We could wear pink blazers. We could land easily in New Mexico. The Wal-Mart parking-lot where all things intersect. Merna's eyes are wide and tight, lighted only occasionally as we pass beneath streetlights. The corner of her eyelash and beyond that, the window, the snow out there, bright somehow beneath the firs. "Should we wake Gramps when we get home?" I ask. I lean against the door, my arm a pillow. "Should we?"

"Probably not."

"I sort of want to talk to him."

"Hmm."

"We could make coffee, carry him to the kitchen. Lay him on the table, or span him between two chairs. We could discuss politics or something. He could tell stories, about the war, about Mom, you know. We could go somewhere. Drive cross-country. He could sleep in the back."

Merna clicks her tongue. "Gramps needs his sleep."

"But."

"Just let him sleep."

"Fine."

I suddenly want something and I feel the want in my stomach, my intestines, my brain, but this thing that I want, I don't know what it is. I try to picture it with my brain and then my eyes. My brain and eyes fail. I stare at my fingernails and ask them what I want. They don't know. The car-window doesn't know. The car doesn't know. I'm doomed to want things that aren't things. The car-window's cold and my cheek's cold and outside's dark and frozen. Merna drives. Does Merna know? Could she place me carefully before it? Carry me piggy-back to the place where the thing I want is? Sit cross-legged there with me, eyes closed?

FORTY-ONE

"I want a motorcycle," I said. "I want a llama."

I sat on the couch between Merna and Anastasia. It was night. There were many lamps.

"I want Monopoly and Operation."

"Monopoly's terrible," Merna said. "It teaches accumulation."

"What's accumulation?" Anastasia asked.

"Nothing."

"Bet you don't know."

Anastasia wore her pink flower-print dress and sat cross-legged with her tiny hands holding tiny knees. Merna's hair was long and wavy, draped thinly over thin shoulders. I wiggled my toes and watched my wiggling toes. A tall man entered the room. He was bald and wore a gray flannel suit with a bright white shirt and a black embroidered tie. A wide overcoat hung from his shoulders, fluttered around his calves. He moved quickly and smoothly, seeming to flicker from one place to another. I gasped, leaned into the couch. Merna combed her hair from her face and held it bunched behind her. Anastasia sobbed once, punctuatingly. The man stood, cliff-like and menacing in a nondescript way, monolithic, projecting a strange foreboding that at once felt omnipresent and source-less. His thin rectangular lips parted softly and I could see the pale tips of his white teeth, each tooth unnaturally straight and parallel. "This," the man said, holding out his hand, palm up. The hand was flat but finely grooved. My eyes traced the grooves and I imagined Lisbon. If Lisbon were in New Mexico, or Alaska. Bill Murray there with Grandfather, draped carefully in American flags. Parking-lots, great sheets of ice. The man's fingers were focused and defined, but the room, the man himself, walls, furniture, posters, all seemed faded, washed-out, gray and formless. I imagined carefully removing the hand with a scalpel, mounting it to driftwood, a trophy with smooth groomed nails, tiny black finger-hairs. Polish the hand. Build a museum for it, hand-museum with a thousand hands, polished and dusted daily, protected in thick glass cases. Admission-fee, guided tour. "This is the tall man's hand," I would say, or "This hand ate other hands." A history of hands, hand-replicas hidden in mystery-boxes, felt-lined holes. "Just feel the hand, whose is it, do you think?" I wanted to touch the hand, to dust it, to eat and absorb the hand, become the hand, to hold the hand with the hand, form it into a fist. "This," he said again.

Anastasia stood.

Merna's head rested on the couch-arm. Her eyes were closed.

"You don't know what 'this' means," Anastasia said. "You're 'this.'"

"Look," he said. He pointed. "This."

"Don't," I said. "Sit, Anastasia." I stood.

"Where?" Anastasia asked.

He pointed. "This."

"Don't," I said. "Sit quietly on the couch with me. Close your eyes."

"I don't see." Anastasia moved her face close to the wall and touched the wall.

"Here," the man said. He held out his finely grooved hand. "This."

"Lisbon," I said. "No."

"This," the man said. He touched Anastasia. "This."

I closed my eyes tightly.

FORTY-TWO

"No," I say. "That's wrong."

"What?"

"Wrong."

Merna has parked the car and we're walking up the driveway. Snow's slowly falling again. The motion-sensor senses our motion. We blink.

"Let's get inside," Merna says. "Do you have the key? My key only opens the back-door."

"No key. No."

I follow Merna along the narrow run between houses and Merna's indistinct before me. My feet and hands are numb and somehow prickly. Inside, we collapse onto my bed which creaks thinly. I yawn. My drapes are drawn and I want suddenly to open them but I'm afraid to move.

"This bed's not soft," Merna says. "Not soft at all."

"Soft beds injure kids. Thousands crippled every year, arthritis or something. Arthritic five-year-olds in the emergency room, strapped to gurneys, irradiated. Know what I mean?"

"My bed's very soft."

"Which is why you're so bent-over, super-curved. Your birth canal's a roller-coaster."

Merna yawns.

"Your babies'll have curved spines, wavy foreheads, because of your bed. S-shaped family. And you'll be sad for a while, then defiant. Deformed. Dangerous."

Merna doesn't answer.

"We should wake Grandpa," I say. "It's practically morning anyway."

"Hmm."

"He probably went to sleep at like six o'clock."

"I wonder what Noah's doing."

"Grandpa could tell me why it's wrong," I say. "I don't know why it's wrong."

"What're you talking about?" Merna rolls onto her side and stares at the wall, holding her hair behind her head. "Noah's probably tired. Maybe he's sleeping. I could call him?"

"Fuck Noah," I say.

"He's at the hospital. He's helping people or something. Or sleeping."

"Anastasia," I say quietly.

"Oh." Merna stands slowly. "This."

"I was thinking about Anastasia."

Merna points her eyes at my eyes. I'm watching Merna's dark shadowy back, her dark shadowy hair, held carefully behind her as she glides through the bedroom-door. Stairs creak. Once. Twice. I want to know the difference between Merna and New Mexico. Merna could be the nexus of all things. Could I enter Merna? I turn onto my side and watch my alarm clock which is orange and bright. I imagine a soft snow-sound, then a thin cold smell that makes me think of leaves. The snow-sound's a crunching but faded, distant. Snow in New Mexico. Lisbon there, the Lisbon Wal-Mart. We're cross-legged on a blanket, the million flags before us. No trees, but leaves everywhere. I imagine a leaf very curved and fetal. I imagine a complex zigzagging wrinkle. My own wrinkle. All wrinkles. Frost crystals.

FORTY-THREE

Anastasia lay on my bedroom floor. Merna snored noisily in her own room down the hall. "Snore," I said. I laughed. Anastasia didn't laugh. I wanted Anastasia to laugh. I wanted to tell her to laugh, to demonstrate laughing, to provide her with an instruction manual. "I want a goat or a cow," I said. "I want a pet, maybe, a jumbo-pet, hairy or shaggy, savable, a horse maybe, something from the zoo. A pet that would usually be food, slave-labor or something. I could make it not-food with bows and ribbons, keep it in the backyard with hay, maybe we need a bigger yard, like a big field, a mini-world, a thousand buffalo, bison, I think." Anastasia was braiding quietly three thin strands of hair. I continued, "We could steal a cow and keep it in the backyard. Feed it grass and clover or something. Take it for walks. Cow-bell. I don't know." Anastasia wore her pink flower-print dress. Outside, bright snowflakes slowly fell. A tall man silently entered the room, flickering. He held out his hand, palm up. Grooved, I thought.

"I want something else now," Anastasia said. "What are you?"

The man shook his head. "This." He walked carefully into the far corner of my bedroom and, facing the corner, rested his dark elliptical head inside the corner and placed his hands on adjacent walls. The fingers were splayed and long and sharp. My hands seemed small and clumsy and I wanted suddenly to remove my fingers with garden-shears. "This," the man said.

Anastasia moved toward him.

"No, Anastasia," I said. "Stay here."

Anastasia pulled the man's gray-flannel blazer. "What are you?"

"This," he said. "This."

Merna's head appeared in my doorway. "Hey, quiet down, now. Cheerleading tryouts tomorrow and I need rest, okay? I don't want dark circles or anything."

"But," I said.

"Don't be a bitch, okay. Just for tonight."

"Anastasia," I said. I pointed.

The man cried quietly in the corner. Anastasia sat cross-legged near his feet.

"Just be quiet, okay?"

"But."

"Complete silence."

Merna's head disappeared.

"Anastasia," I said. "Anastasia," I said again.

FORTY-FOUR

My cell-phone ring-tone makes me think of burning slow-motion children at recess, or on the jungle-gym, or thirty-five-thousand dwarves marching carefully through tall and rugged grass-blades or across endless concrete expanses. I open my cell-phone and place my cell-phone near my ear and my ear hears ragged digitized breathing. Then, "My head." It's Erik. More breathing. "Aaron stabbed me or something. He stabbed my abdomen, I think, he might have stabbed my chest or neck." I'm silent. "Or punched my eye. He could've punched my eye and mouth and broke my teeth. There's some blood, I think. A little blood. Call the police, you should call the police. You should call someone to clean up the blood. There's a lot of it. It'll stain something. I'm afraid of staining things. There's something. I mean." I'm holding the phone to my ear, my body motionless. "My legs are broken." The breathing's less ragged now. "Are you home? Should I come to the apartment? I want to play Nintendo or something, together."

"I'm somewhere else." I roll onto my back and shut my eyes. "You're injured? Shouldn't you go to the emergency-room? Call 911 or something? Ambulance and police."

"I'm okay."

"But you're bleeding."

"Only a little. It's okay now. Where are you? I can show you my stab-wounds and stuff."

"I'm sleeping. I'm okay."

"I should be sleeping with you. We're partners, after all. You left your watch at Denny's, you know. You're lucky I found it. I'll bring it to you."

"I don't have a watch."

"No?" Erik says. "Come meet me. Come to the mall. The mall parking-lot."

"I'm really tired." I yawn loudly. "We'll talk tomorrow."

"Meet me at Wal-Mart. I'll call Aaron. We can have a conference."

"I'd prefer not to."

"We have plane-tickets for you. To Lisbon. Flight leaves in three hours. You must go to Lisbon immediately."

"I'm turning off my phone."

"But we love you. We need to see you. To take you to Lisbon." I'm sighing, holding the cell-phone away from my face. "Come to Wal-Mart." Erik's voice's high-pitched and desperate. I want only to sleep now, maybe for weeks, here in this bed. I want never to see or think of Erik, of his shiny red face, his silly late-night phone-calls. Flags. Nintendo. I could never go to New Mexico, to Lisbon. Lie next to him. "We'll rob the Wal-Mart if you don't come. Take hostages. Murder cashiers. Please help. Stop us, please."

I turn off my cell-phone and place the cell-phone on my nightstand. I remember buying the nightstand at a garage-sale. "Needs to be refinished," Grandfather said to the woman. "We'll give you a nickel."

The woman was old and wrinkled. Her fingers were thin, twisted, rigid. She was moving to a rest-home in New Mexico. She nodded, held out her hand. I gave her the nickel. My grandfather lifted the nightstand.

I can't sleep, so I walk downstairs.

Grandfather carried the nightstand upstairs. He wiped it slowly with a rag.

I watch my feet as I walk and my feet are small and bare and narrow but flat and hard so that I can barely feel the floor with them. Could the nightstand feel the floor? How do objects feel? Is the nightstand different than Grandfather? It's possible that Grandfather's somehow the nightstand, that they are the same. There's a light in the kitchen. I move to the light. Merna and Stepmother sit at the kitchen-table. There's coffee. The floor's cold.

"Good morning," Stepmother says. "Sit." I look at the clock. Two AM. I watch my feet which are small and tight and aligned with the polished wood floor. I make my feet touch my feet.

"We should wake Grandpa," I say. "We can have group insomnia, play Monopoly or something. I'll build slum-motels on Baltic."

"Come sit with us," Merna says. "Leave Grandpa alone."

Stepmother lays her head on the table. The head's round and thin and the hair on the head's tangled and frizzy and I want to comb the hair, straighten the hair, make the hair orderly and calm, maybe braid it into one perfect hair-rope. I sit. It's late and early and today and tomorrow and my shoulders are tight and pained as though each shoulder-muscle and each shoulder-tendon are tensed and tied or maybe webbed and netted, and I imagine my netted musculature strung between cars with little neighborhood-dogs caught in the muscle-net and stuck to the muscle-web and waiting sadly to be rescued or to die.

Merna's hand touches my shoulder and we're touching slowly and tenderly. Strange and human, I think. Strangely, I think. "Human," I say.

"You're my sister," Merna says. "I'm sorry."

FORTY-FIVE

I was in the family-room, braiding my hair.

"You're my sisters," Merna said. "I'm sorry."

The tall man walked carefully into the far corner of the family-room and, facing the corner, rested his dark elliptical head inside the corner and placed his hands flat on adjacent walls. The fingers were splayed and long and sharp. The man laughed slowly, quietly.

We ignored him.

Anastasia lay between us.

Grandfather sat in his recliner, reading. He set his newspaper on his lap. "We should go to Portugal sometime," he said. "You'd like that wouldn't you. We could buy a small deli and make grilled-cheese sandwiches and sell them, live in a small farmhouse with three dogs, a goat."

"Maybe," I said.

"Portugal," Anastasia said.

"Yes," Grandfather said. "Lisbon."

FORTY-SIX

"In my comic-book Bill Murray will model crescent-moon leotards, in Albuquerque maybe," I say. "In a small white room, on the dust jacket, Bill Murray twirling a little baton. I wouldn't sleep. My head would be small and thin, question-marks instead of facial-features." I imagine fleshy question-mark facial-features. How would I see? Would it matter? "Call me Question, sleepless interrogator of super-villains." Stepmother's face-down on the kitchen-table, her fingers laced over her head, softly holding the head against the table, her hair soft and white, plumping around her fingers. "Ever think about Anastasia?" I ask her. "Sometimes I want to ask simply everyone. Especially cashiers. I've been dreaming of her lately. I wonder why I dream about things. She's walking around in my dreams, walking on asphalt, steadily climbing toward a flat place."

There's a silence.

"I'm pregnant," Merna says.

"What?" Stepmother says.

"You'll be a great-grandmother."

"Great-grand-step-mother-person," I say. "Anastasia," I say quietly and to no one in particular. Could we name them Anastasia? Anastasia One and Two?

"Twins," Merna says. "We've been trying for years. I have a DVD of the ultrasound, a boy and girl, we think. I'll show it, you know. We'll watch the DVD. Noah says we shouldn't name them yet, until they're complete, independently alive, because people with names are different than people without names, maybe. I don't know. There are too many names."

"Wonderful." Stepmother raises her head. She's crying.

"You should name them Anastasia. Anastasia's a good name," I say. Merna's watching me. "That's what I'd name them, even if they were boys."

Merna smiles her wide flat smile and cradles her stomach, which seems strange and round, both larger and smaller than before, rounder, a globe, motionless. I want to rub her stomach, to caress it, to feel her stomach through her stomach, baby-feet, hands, heads, moving there beneath the stomach. How small are the different parts? I want to experience this smallness, for my hands and fingers to shrink, my arms, feet, to look at them from a distance, to lay them flat on blankets in a parking-lot, determine then their value. "Why don't we wake Grandpa?" I ask. "I'm sure he'd want to hear about twins. Probably has a thousand twin-names. Ten-thousand." I imagine my hand wrapped around Grandfather's ankle, my body splayed beneath his bed, the room dark and cold. "Anarchy," I would shout. "Anything can happen." Which is hilarious somehow, but I lock my laughter carefully away. In middle-school I laughed aloud during a history lecture. After class, the teacher told me to wait by her desk. When we were alone she asked if laughter was appropriate. I didn't answer. She began a list on the whiteboard:

ethnic cleansing
rape
genocide
murder
class struggle
melamine milk
nuclear bombs
Hiroshima
Darfur

"Laugh at that, I dare you," she said. "History's not funny." But I did laugh. Grandfather came for me. He was laughing. He took me home. We sat here in the kitchen.

"We could trick him," I say. "We could take him out in the snow."

"Stop it," Merna says.

Stepmother stands and turns away. Her bathrobe's thick and long and white, folded and shadowy, and I want the bathrobe to be my bathrobe, for Stepmother to be me. Or to be Grandfather, to shuffle carefully down the stairs, into the family-room, to sit there next to Stepmother, to pat her lowered head. I might say, "I had that Martian-moon-dream with you and Anastasia and everyone, then the gigantic minivan one, in Montana, became rich selling pimentos to Canadians." Or maybe, "Let's go to Lisbon for the summer. Read books, live under hotel-buffets, highjack Snickers freight-trucks at night or something, dump them in ravines." But Grandfather's not there and I'm not him and nobody's saying anything.

"Listen," Merna says.

I'm standing. I'm walking.

"Come walk with me," Merna says. "Outside, in the snow or something."

"No thanks," I say.

Merna grabs my arm. "Seriously. We should go to the grocery-store for something, soda maybe. I'll buy you a soda."

I can see my step-grandmother and she's rocking quietly in the dark, her hands folded on her lap. "We should turn on a lamp," I say. I feel reckless. "We should break all the lamps and make a lamp-pile, light it on fire."

"Come on. Orange soda?"

"Lamp-fire's a dumb idea. You're right. That's a dumb idea."

"We could climb out on the roof again."

"Let's watch TV or something, every lamp everywhere on."

"Just leave her alone."

"Who wants to be alone?" Merna's holding my arm and pulling my arm. "We could play Monopoly or something. I could be a real-estate power-broker. Evict you. Build Wal-Marts instead of hotels." Step-grandmother stretches her body across the couch, closes her eyes. In the lamp-less family-room, she's thin and dark, sinister in a filmic way, a sleepy assassin, a serial killer. She's stern and quiet, still, carefully deciding my human-fate, how to murder me, who to hire, what kind of death I should die. Or what kind of death all people should die. What to do with the bodies, how to dress the bodies before the burning. Each funeral a pageant. Grandfather with her behind the lectern. The parking-lot stretching into the distance, heat rising wavy through the air. Each of us touching every other one of us.

FORTY-SEVEN

"Who's saying the eulogy?" I asked.

"I am," Grandfather answered. "I wrote this thing about pimentos."

"What's a pimento?"

"I don't know." We were sitting in Grandfather's Cadillac. There was sun. I was small and my toes were small and I watched my toes and wiggled my toes and felt the smallness of them. They seemed like tiny independent ants, beetles maybe. With the right pressure, would my toes pop? "Use your power-windows," Grandfather said. "Make the buzzing sound." He was laughing. "Buzz," he said. "Buzz buzz buzz." I used the power-windows. "Very good," he said.

"I'm a skilled employee."

"And I'm a skilled employer. We're a good team. I'll find the capital. You do the backbreaking labor."

"I'll steal a car or something, take it to a chop-shop. Sell the car-pieces, open a car-piece shop to fund my gambling ring."

"Okay, very good." Grandfather hunched over the steering-wheel. His profile was large and jagged. The Cadillac's interior was bright and filmy and everywhere the air was suffused with sparkles or dust motes which slowly moved at angles, adjacent from all things. Grandfather's face was deep and wrinkled and his mouth was very serious and straight and even his teeth were serious and straight and calm and I knew suddenly that one day I too would have a serious calm mouth and one day a girl would look at my serious calm mouth and would think to herself that one day she too would have this same serious calm mouth. "Listen," Grandfather said. "I have to be serious."

I wanted his teeth. Very straight. Mine were crooked, ready to fall out. I could reach in, take just one tooth, two. I imagined it. Put them in my mouth. "Listen," I said.

"You'll stay with us. We've decided. I've made all the necessary arrangements and we have plenty of room and there are good schools here. I want you and Merna here. We want you."

"I'll stay." I didn't know what to say, only that I was supposed to say something.

"You and Merna." Grandfather watched the road ahead. There was a stoplight. "We moved your stuff already. We'll play Monopoly forever, or Chess, Chutes and Ladders, something. I know it's not, or can't be the same, or similar anymore. It'll be quiet. Comfortable. People will only talk when they want to. You and your grandmother can decorate a little. We'll go to the zoo. You like the zoo? I like penguins. I like the giraffes because they're very tall. It can be similar or the same, maybe. There will be penguins. I'm sure of that."

"Same."

"It can't be the same, but it can be okay."

"Okay," I said.

Grandfather nodded. "Chutes and Ladders," he said.

"Chutes and Ladders," I said.

FORTY-EIGHT

"Chutes."

The front-porch is wide and white and cold. There are stars. Merna stands next to me. Our breath heats the air, steaming, and the steam's amorphous and fog-like until it disappears.

"Ladders," Merna says.

"Do you ever imagine the world or reality, like downtown or high school, or the hospital or whatever, based on a Chutes and Ladders system?" Merna doesn't answer. "Like you're walking downtown and a ladder appears before you and you climb the ladder because when ladders appear you must climb them and you're walking again and there's a tall man in front of you and you're approaching the man and suddenly the man disappears. The man's there and not there. You approach. There's a chute. You stand in front of the chute and wonder if you should slide down the chute." I imagine the man standing on the front-porch, his head resting in a corner, hands flat against adjacent walls. The man is there. "Do you slide down the chute? Where does it take you?"

"Listen, I have to tell you something."

"But it's a chute and the chute's very red and deep and this red chute curves slightly, disappears—but you've stopped in font of the chute so you must slide down the chute and there's nothing else to be done but close your eyes and slide." The man is not there.

"We used to play Chutes and Ladders."

"I cheated."

"Doesn't matter." Merna's watching my face.

"Cheating's the only way to win. That's why I cheat. I'm a cheater." The man is there, the chute is there.

"Listen, it's about Grandpa."

"The chute's there and not there." I imagine the chute and the chute's there.

FORTY-NINE

If I designed my own people, I'd make all human-angles sharp, knife-like—chins, elbows, knees, noses, fingers, all would end in points. People would embrace one another carefully, at substantial risk to their health and well-being. I'm in the bathroom. Six soft-white light-bulbs arc over the bathroom-mirror. I'm in the mirror and I'm here. The mirror softly reflects the low white toilet, the fogged shower-door. I touch the shower-door and it's cool and I'm envious of the shower-door because my skin's always warm and uncomfortable. I wish my skin were made from shower-doors. I wish my face were glass. "Chutes and Ladders," I say aloud. "People."

There's a knock on the door. "Are you in there?" It's Merna.

I wonder who you is. "I'm me," I say, "and I'm here." There's another knock. "I'm sorry," I say to the door. I open the door. Shower-door knife-skin. Merna's standing very still with her hands hanging loosely at her side. "I'm me," I say. "I'm sorry." My cell-phone ring-tone's playing a song. "Here." I hand my cell-phone to Merna. "Answer it." Merna holds the cell-phone and looks at the cell-phone in her hand. "It's a cellular-telephone," I say.

Merna pushes a button. "Hello," she says. I step into the hallway. "Oh hi," Merna says. "What do you want?"

"Who is it?" I say.

"Very funny."

"What's funny?"

Merna hands me the cell-phone. "Talk."

I hold the cell-phone against my face.

"I'm at the airport." It's Aaron's voice. I imagine Aaron at the airport and I picture his round wide body standing very still on a narrow conveyor-belt. Is the conveyor moving? Merna operating the conveyor. Bill Murray and Erik shopping slowly for a chess-set at the kiosk. Bill Murray lying quietly on the conveyor, arms crossed over his chest. There's no chess-set. The airport's closed. Aaron always on the conveyor, moving from one place to another. Empty airport. Grainy security cameras. Everyone on an escalator that stops. "Why am I here?" Aaron asks. "What am I supposed to be doing?" I grunt but don't answer. Merna moves her head near my head so she can hear. Aaron's voice wavers as he continues. "I think I love you or something." There's a long pause. "Come to the airport. Come meet me. Come to Wal-Mart. Meet at the Wal-Mart parking-lot. Buy you a ticket to somewhere. Lisbon. We'll go."

"I can't." There are one-million Wal-Marts. Which one could he mean? Everywhere could be Wal-Mart. Are Wal-Mart and Aaron the same? I feel nervous and imagine conveyors of cartons moving slowly into Wal-Mart. Forklifts, each driven by Aaron. Noah and Merna there, the twins in cartons. Each person designing their own personal carton, packing themselves then in styrofoam popcorn. The sky's cloudless and cold and blue. There's a biplane. I want there to be a system that defines Aaron. I want there to be honeycombs of people, packaged carefully together, each carton touching every other carton.

Aaron's talking.

"You're not Bill Murray," I say.

"What?"

"I'm trapped in a parking-lot or something." I turn off my cell-phone and sit quietly in the hallway. I lean against the wall. The wall's solid and cold. I'm cold. "Merna," I say. I tell Merna I'm cold. I tell Merna about parking-lots.

FIFTY

There are old stained-couches, a dirty piano, and a large heavy television. I sit on one couch. Merna sits on another. The television teaches us about steak-knives that never need sharpening. "I wish I had those knives," I say. "I'd cut a watermelon in half and in half again, until there was only watermelon pulp. I'd carve a cow. I'd chop a cement-block." Merna doesn't answer. She pulls her long thin hair through her fingers, then back behind her shoulders and holds it solidly there. She knots her fingers in her hair and the hair tangles and bends and twist around Merna's finger-joints like a vine-y plant. "I'd pin baby-rabbits to the kitchen wall," I say. "I'd slice rebar like butter." There are commercials. On television, a tall man walks slowly across a darkened bedroom and stands quietly in the corner, his hands flat against adjacent walls. His elliptical head rests in the corner. "Merna," I say. I'm pointing.

Merna's talking into her cell-phone. "Noah," she says. She says something else.

"Merna," I say. I'm pointing. I listen.

"...a few days...be with Grandma. Just...okay...." Merna holds her cell-phone away from her face. "Dog died," she tells me. "Nothing anybody could do." The commercial changes and the tall man slowly fades. The phone's next to Merna's face. I want to move my face nearby.

"...my sister. Watching television. Can't sleep...too tired...too strange, unsettled..."

I call Erik's cell-phone with my cell-phone but it goes straight to voicemail. After the beep, I say, "I'm in this parking-lot atop Mount Everest. There are five thousand SUVs, a million people filming me while I load groceries into my little Honda and I've been stabbed I think and am bleeding but am too scared to say anything and I feel a little embarrassed about the blood that's staining my new white-blouse." I turn off my cell-phone. Outside it's still night, but the sky's changed from black to dark-gray and where there were clouds, there are now stars and somewhere the moon, but from here on this stained-couch and through the low half-window that peeks just above the snow, I can't see the moon. "Merna," I say. "I'm sorry. I did it. I stabbed him for five years, drained his blood into little jars. I stored them in the garage in the big freezer." Merna's silent. "I amputated fingers and toes, hands and feet, forearms, shins, kneecaps, elbows, any other pieces I could imagine amputating, framed them, took them to show-and-tell. When I went to glue them back together the pieces didn't fit, had changed." I close my eyes. I want something now. My chest hurts and my arms hurt, and my hands feel as though they're reaching and closing and wanting and grasping and there's something somewhere that my hands want to hold and keep, to absorb and become. I'm watching my hands and my hands are opening and closing. I think, Anastasia. I think something else. There's a boat but it's not a boat and I'm not on the boat because the boat's empty. There is a boat, I think to myself. It's filled with mud. "I have to go upstairs," I say. "Come on. We'll go together. But we have to do something. We always

195

have to do something." I feel as though I'm failing. "Upstairs," I say.

"Okay."

"Upstairs," I say again.

I wonder if I want to fail. I wonder how I'd know.

FIFTY-ONE

The stairs were thin and narrow and between them tiny shoots of grass had grown so that from a distance the stairs appeared no different than the hill they climbed. The stairs were stone, ruined, and each time I placed my foot on one I felt it might suddenly crumble. But no stair crumbled and slowly we made our way to the top of the hill where the land was flat and grassy. "Parking-lot," Grandfather said. Father was laughing. It was quiet.

"Are we there?" Anastasia asked. "Or somewhere, anyway?"

There was a blanket in my backpack and Grandfather removed the blanket and spread the blanket smooth and wide over a brown patch of grass at the top of the stairs. We sat cross-legged on the blanket and shared a bag of potato-chips. There was wind. "Where are we?" I asked.

"Lisbon." Grandfather held a handful of potato-chips. "Might be Wisconsin. Probably Lisbon and Wisconsin simultaneously, like a time/space-warp, but no way to test. Could build a little hut here, grow a garden with broccoli and carrots and apples, peas. Eat leaves and grass. Climb trees. Or build huts in the trees. Hide rope/net traps. Snares. They're called snares, I think. Kidnap all the pirates and free Lisbon/Wisconsin, once and for all from the pirate menace."

Anastasia and Father went for a walk.

Grandfather curled up on the blanket and fell asleep. I stood over him and watched his face which was worn and wrinkled and small and framed by the wide collar of his plain white dress-shirt. Asleep, he appeared eye-less and warm, plain and calm, wrinkled everywhere so that his skin seemed worn and loose. I moved my face close to Grandfather's face until I could feel the microscopic edges of his stubble. I sat cross-legged next to Grandfather's curled body until the sky darkened. With wide-open eyes, I said, "You're a person." Nothing answered. I watched the stairs but there were no stairs and my brain told me the stairs were not stairs but people now old and dead and curled carefully against the side of the hill.

FIFTY-TWO

"How would you design people?" I ask Merna. "If you designed people?" Merna doesn't answer. We're in the hallway and there are many doors, some of them open. The hallway's dark and gray and the doors and walls and light-fixtures are thin gray forms that move slowly at the edge of my eyes, but not really the edge because my eyes have no edge. We're standing in front of a closed door and Merna's hand's on the doorknob. "I'd make people sharp," I say. "I'd make people very small, efficient so that each movement was perfect. Everyone in points. People would be ant-sized, always useful in some way. So small it would be difficult to destroy things, or even to change them. People wouldn't be people. They'd be something else."

"I don't want to talk right now."

"People are supposed to talk. People have mouths."

"I don't want to."

"Would you design them without mouths?"

Merna opens the door. We step into the room. The bed's wide and long, almost filling the room. Thick checkered quilts cover the bed, overlapping somehow. I walk sideways, shuffling, my knees brushing the side of the bed, pulling the quilts awkwardly. I hold my knees away from the bed and arc my body in a precarious and unbalanced way. I touch the bed with my hands and remove my hands and hold my hands at my sides.

"We're here," Merna says.

"I thought you didn't want to talk."

"Now I want to talk."

"Oh." I watch the bed. Centered on the bed is Grandfather's body and the sheets and quilts are gathered over the top of the body and everything in the room is very still and cold. I place my hand again on the quilts, squeezing them. "This," I say. I stop. I watch Grandfather's face and the face is cold and gray.

"We're here," Merna says. "What do you want to do?"

"I don't know."

"What're you thinking about?"

"I don't know."

"Aren't you thinking?"

"Maybe."

"You should be thinking something," Merna says. "People should think things because being a person is thinking and you're a person."

"What're you thinking?" I ask. "What do you want?" I feel suddenly tired and don't want to know what Merna wants. I don't want to know anything.

"Stop," Merna says.

"I don't want to know anything," I say. "I don't know anything anyway." I sit on the edge of the bed and the bed's cold and I'm cold and I and the bed are cold together. "Miniature-people are better." I feel suddenly that I want to kiss Grandfather's face and in my mind I see my face kissing Grandfather's face deeply and I'm nervous and cold and hug myself because I've never kissed Grandfather and I know I shouldn't now because it'd be inappropriate but the image is there even when I close my eyes.

"I have to go," Merna says. Merna goes.

I sit quietly for a while. I imagine kissing Grandfather.

FIFTY-THREE

Pale light filters through my bedroom shutters. It's cold and quiet and when I exhale a thin white fog appears. I watch the fog and it's formless and wet. I watch my hands and my hands open and close. I sit on my bed. I stand. I sit on my bed again, folding carefully my quilt. My bed's cold and unmade, narrow and lumpy. I'm yawning. I'm holding my sheet. There's a soreness in the middle of my back that I want to touch. To move the soreness, to my face maybe. I consider sleeping. I stand and walk. "Where am I walking?" I say aloud. Nobody answers. I'm outside. I'm in my neighborhood. There are trees and white houses. Each house is the same house with the same three floors, foyers, picture-windows, white shutters. "Something, something," I say to myself. The sky's gray and grainy and backlighted distantly. I'm on a hilltop. I'm near an empty Honda. There's a stoplight. I stop. A dirty pickup pulls up, pink racing stripe spattered with mud. Inside the pickup a boy yawns. The boy's face is dark and wet and hairy, the hair curled and dirty, the face wide and smiling. "Why are you smiling?" I ask. I move toward the pickup. The boy shakes his head, still smiling, wet lips hidden by the beard. I wheel my hand as though rolling down a window. The boy rolls down his window. "Why's your face smiling like that?"

"Don't know," the boy says. He touches his face. "My face?"

"It's cold here."

"It is."

"Then why smile?" I feel angry. The boy's smiling without reason or logic. To smile when the air's cold is wrong, stupid probably. "Why? Don't you consider the cold? Or that other people might be cold, uncomfortable?"

"The snow's very beautiful today," the boy says. He touches the snow on the roof of his car. "I like it. I like the snow." I watch the boy's face and it still smiles but the smile has become confused, strange. I want to wear this smile. I move my mouth experimentally but there's no mirror and I feel nervous and hideous and self-aware. The boy drums the pickup-door. "I have to go, okay." The boy's gone. I follow but slowly. I'm in a strip-mall. I'm near an AM/PM. I go in the AM/PM.

"Hello," the clerk says.

"Can I use your phone?"

"Do you ever think about telephones?" The clerk leans over the counter. "Personally, I don't use telephones because who knows how they're mutating our bodies. Through our ears, right? Who wants to talk so much anyway? It's immoral. Personally, I hate talking and would destroy telephone technology if I could. Televisions, everything. All tele-things." I make my face blank. "Don't buy stuff from this store." His knuckles whiten on the counter. I watch them, wonder if they'll change. "It's the movement I started, the 'don't buy stuff here' movement. Listen: ever think about where this shit comes from? Like, I haven't researched it or anything, but probably this shit's imported from communist and fascist regimes whose primary focus, I'm sure, is to prevent the free-flow of ideas

203

on television and to keep prime-time American broadcasting away from their brain-washed citizens. China, for example. Who knows what's in this shit? Lead. Melamine. Strychnine."

"What?"

"AM/PM purchases are unpatriotic and sinful, which is basically the same thing." The clerk's face contorts strangely, his mouth round and jagged. "All proceeds go to support fascio-communist global-terrorism." I watch the clerk's face, unsure of what to say. "You can buy beer though. Beer is one-hundred percent American."

"What about telephones?"

"What do you mean? We don't sell telephones." His face becomes very loose and worn, raggedly hanging, as though it might drip free. He sits carefully on a tall round stool.

"Telephone technology? Talking?"

"I don't understand."

"We're talking now."

"Are you going to buy some beer or not?" I don't answer. "Maybe you're the fascist. Maybe that's why you won't buy the beer, fascist." I sit on the floor. Am I a fascist, or a communist? Am I both? I watch my hands for clues. "You can't just sit there, commie. Buy something or go." The clerk crosses his arms in front of his chest. His forearms seem very large and menacing. My arms are small, thin. When I cross them, nothing happens. The clerk's face is knotted, mottled somehow. Red. "I could call the police to arrest you for stealing because you are stealing. You'd be arrested, put in a little cell. You'd stay there for like forty years which is what fascio-commies deserve. No trial by peers. Nothing. We'd get shit done if I ran things. No more coddling commies." I go to the cooler and select a can of beer and return. "Good choice," the clerk says. "Domestic." He takes my money. I go outside. I drink my beer. There's sun and clouds. I'm walking and as I walk my legs and feet feel energetic and warm. There's wind on my face and I'm moving very fast. There are other people but I'm passing them. They're slow-moving and red, mired in the ankle-deep snow. Cars appear, and a snow-plow. There's a soft crunching everywhere. The snow becomes dirty and warm, slushy. My feet are wet through my shoes. I'm at Wal-Mart. I carefully set my beer-can next to the sliding-door. I go inside. It's warm and there are thousands of people and each person's moving comfortably, pushing shopping-carts. An old man holds a bikini. A girl rolls on her heels while her mother browses the bras. I stand near the televisions. Each television plays the same movie with the same grazing deer, its eyes black and wide, unblinking. The deer's motionless, vacant, focused on the brown grass. Somewhere there's a hunter.

"Welcome to Wal-Mart," a voice says. "In the market for a new television, because, let me tell you, we have the most comprehensive variety of televisions in the western hemisphere."

"That sounds like a lie."

"Let me level with you," the voice says. "It is a lie. A teeny one. But I thought if I said it energetically you'd want a television. Everyone knows that sales-people are supposed to lie anyway, like Olympic sprinters."

"Oh."

"You know, Olympic sprinters use HGH, blood-transfusions, anything. They want to win gold medals, to be the fastest person which isn't as fast as a car but pretty fast for a person."

"You want to win?"

"Maybe. Maybe I'm bored." The voice adjusts its red vest. "They don't give gold medals for television sales," the voice whispers. "Not even bronze medals."

"I want a television," I say.

"Really?"

"I want to destroy the television."

"Oh. Okay. Cool." The voice's red vest's dirty and in the vest-pockets are dozens of black ballpoint pens. I open my mouth but don't speak. The voice walks away. I want Merna here. I consider calling her. I would say, "We are humans." Merna next to me at Wal-Mart. We could take the G.I. Joes somewhere. I see a swinging-door and walk through it. I'm in a warehouse. "Hey," a voice says. "You can't be here."

I nod. "No," I say. "You are correct." I run. I'm near a shelf. I'm behind the shelf and between large brown boxes. I'm musty and I'm the box and I'm inside the box because I'm what the box holds. I think about dwarves in a warehouse. Dwarves in boxes, holding rolled coins. Dwarves making my own box, packing me with styrofoam popcorn. All of the angles are sharp. We're hugging, bleeding slowly on the concrete. There's blood everywhere. It's so embarrassing. How would we clean the blood? The flags folded on a blanket. Erik there, wiping the blood with Merna. Merna's not a towel. Not a towel.

The voice with the red vest returns. "What are you doing here?" it asks.

"Thinking," I say.

The voice sits next to me. "Are you thinking about television?"

"No."

"Neither was I."

"Oh."

"Here," the voice says. It hands me a sharpie. "Write slogans with this, like 'eat me and support Canadian apartheid' or 'Jesus something something video-games!' I like that one. I made that one up by myself." I watch the voice. "It's what I do most of the time, when I'm not selling TVs."

"Erik," another voice says.

I make myself small.

"Erik," the new voice says again. "Mr. X's looking for you." The voice's laughing. "Mr. X has a mission." The new voice moves its head side to side in a nervous way then shuffles quickly out the double-doors. I watch the original voice and it's very concentrated, hunched over boxes, writing slogans darkly, repeatedly, re-tracing and re-designing the slogans until the slogans are jagged and smeared. One says, 'Cannibalism is the only reasonable alternative to fossil-fuel.' Another says, 'Robot-people are robot-people too, probably.' I stand and walk. Above me are rows of fluorescent light-tubes. Behind me the voice's still writing slogans on boxes, his body bent awkwardly, his hands clutching a sharpie. I touch my face and it's blank and formless. I'm moving and the fluorescent lights buzz above. I'm thinking about windows. Opening and closing. There are faces. I move beyond them. I'm on the highway. There's a human. He's very wide, with a small head, long dangling arms. His puffy black rain-parka segments him. The arms move of their own accord. I think for a moment that he's Aaron but Aaron's at the airport. I follow the not-Aaron. If it were Aaron, I'd probably stab it. The not-Aaron moves into a café. I follow. The café's warm and dark with small red tables and plush worn armchairs. I sit. The not-Aaron orders coffee. I wonder if I should order coffee. I don't know. I watch the not-Aaron and it's not Aaron. Its face is narrow and tall, its neck's very thin and sinuous. The head wobbles as it walks. It sits at my table.

"Are you following me?"

"No," I say. I feel tight and ball-like.

"I think you're following me."

"I'm just out for a walk."

"Did someone hire you, the cops?" He drinks from his coffee.

"I'm out for a walk," I say.

"It was a joke," he says. "A practical joke. A small one. I was eating ice-cream. The cops have the receipt. Do you have an arrangement?" Not-Aaron's smiling. "You're very pretty."

"I don't know what you're talking about."

"It was mint-chocolate-chip." His face is very red and lined with puffed-cheeks. Thick round eyeballs bulge a little and sit in the face, motionless. His wide stomach bumps the table. "It was already dead anyway and I found it that way. I needed to eat something." I think about Merna and Anastasia. I think about Grandfather and Aaron and Erik. I imagine them in a minivan, driving through Montana. New Mexico. Driving across the Atlantic to Lisbon. I'm in back atop of a pile of blankets and jackets and I'm watching the empty freeway and Aaron and Erik and Anastasia and Merna and my grandparents are chattering but I can't understand them. I'm touching my ears because my ears are scrambled and warm. I want to hold the ears, to remove them, but I don't know how. He stands and points. "You can't judge me."

"You did it because you wanted to," I say. I don't know why.

"You don't know what you're talking about."

The barista's watching us. I push the table. "You're evil." My face is blank and tense and my body's cold and calm. I feel terrible and sad and I don't know what evil means. I wonder why I say anything. I imagine the minivan, sleeping in the minivan, in Montana or Lisbon. New Mexico, the parking-lots spread out before us. Not-Aaron standing, fisted hands. My own hands. All of us climbing slowly a hill, the stairs crumbling into shale fragments. Thin slices of shale. Streetlights, one by one, begin to light up. We collect the shale slices, lay them out in the back of the minivan, and wonder where we are.

FIFTY-FOUR

There's a minivan in Montana. Montana's in Lisbon, somewhere. New Mexico surrounds everything. There's a tall white house on the highway and there's a basement and in this basement are three stained-couches, a large wood-framed television, and a tall thin man standing quietly in the corner, his hands resting on perpendicular walls.

I am nowhere and not there but I say this anyway: "Who are you?"

"I am," the man says, "this."

He turns his head slightly and the head's wide and pasty and expressionless.

"Why?"

"I'm hungry, maybe. That's all."

I consider this. I consider his mouth and his mouth's wide and toothy and there are too many teeth and the teeth are narrow and white and packed tightly together inside the mouth.

"I haven't eaten. Need to clip my fingernails."

I watch the man's hands and there are no fingernails.

"I need something probably."

"Food?"

"My stomach hurts a little. I'm pale and weak and my hands don't work anymore."

He shows me his hands. He tries to make a fist.

"They're vein-y, with tendonitis, some kind of inflammation. I want my hands to do things they can't. They do other things."

I sit softly on the old stained-couch and my body's solid and wide and couch-like and I feel soft everywhere.

"Don't you understand?" the man says. "This."

He shows me his hand and his hand's very thin with a very narrow unlined palm.

I lie on the couch and the couch's a shopping-cart and I'm moving but I'm here on the stained-couch and very soft. I feel tired. I listen to the sounds but there are no sounds and I wonder where the sounds are.

"You're boring," I say.

The man strangles me for a while.

"Don't do that."

I feel tired and calm.

The man stares in a sad way. His hands are thin and cold and I watch them as they encircle my neck.

"I won't, okay," the man says. "Keep quiet for a while, okay?"

He strangles me and I watch as he strangles me. Behind him the television plays a commercial. A woman with thin blonde hair lathers her pale body with thick white foam and I imagine the soap and the foam in my hands and what I'd do with the soap, who I'd give it to, because I'd give the soap to everyone and they would strangle me for a while, each one taking a turn, until I stand finally and walk naked along the highway with handfuls and handfuls of knives.

FIFTY-FIVE

The café wall's rough and I imagine feeling its individual atoms, interacting with them, my fingers manipulating the atoms until they're different atoms.

"What was that about?" the barista asks. She's the only person in the café.

"I don't know."

"Cool."

The barista leans against the counter in a tired way and sighs through thin half-parted lips. Her face is lined and worn and as the barista leans against the counter each part of her body hangs slackly and I feel suddenly like any part might fall from the body, might lie motionless on the floor. "Would you like some coffee, or a croissant, a blueberry-muffin? I have pastries you know." The barista gestures toward a glass case. "You could have anything you wanted. Like coffee-cake or something. Sorry about before with that guy. He's always sort of dramatic, but he doesn't usually hurt people."

"Usually?"

"Yeah, usually. Only once. Anyway, I can give you free coffee, pastries. It's in my discretionary budget." The barista smiles and stands upright. "Come back here for awhile. What's your name? Don't you like coffee and pastries?"

"Who's the person who usually doesn't hurt people? What's its name?"

"You should try some foamed milk. Sit with me in back. I'm taking a break anyway." The barista edges past me and locks the front door. "Come back here. I have these cheese-curds from Tillamook, they're very good, and free coffee. We'll share the coffee. I like you, I think." I follow the barista down a narrow hallway. There are evenly spaced doors but we pass the doors and turn left at a fork and then right at the next fork. Here the hallway becomes very bright with uncovered halogen light-bulbs. Along the ceiling are long gray pipes of varying diameter and shape. Sometimes a pipe disappears into the ceiling only to reappear a few feet down the hallway. There are many knobs and levers and I want to turn the knobs and pull the levers but I hold my hands quietly at my sides. "Back here," the barista says. She pulls a thin curtain aside and steps into a dirty rectangular room. Centered in the room is a card-table with a checkered cloth. Next to it is a filthy refrigerator. There are no chairs. The ceiling's lined with pipes and valves and levers and knobs. The barista's holding a package of cheese-curds. "They're very good."

"This customer," I say, brushing the cheese-curds aside. "Who'd it hurt?"

"Some woman, it's not important."

"What happened?"

"I said it's not important." The barista puts the cheese-curds away and crosses her arms. "I'm trying to give you stuff. Don't you want free things?"

"Did the customer use a knife, a gun? Or just fists or hands or feet?"

"I told you it's not important." The barista walks back into the hallway. "Come on. You have to go."

"What about the cheese-curds? Coffee?" I sit carefully on the edge of the card-table. I feel strange and warm and want terribly to know everything about the customer. Somehow the customer, Merna, Grandfather, the tall dark man, Anastasia, my parents, me, we're all sitting cross-legged on a blanket, picnicking, sharing grapes, bread and water. A dog's barking and a boat's floating somewhere in the distance, half filled with mud, and there's a tall hill or mountain and we're there, in the parking lot. A little fire's burning quietly. I want to explain this to the barista but the barista's in the hallway, slowly tapping her foot. "Sit with me for a moment so I can think of something to say."

"My break's over." The barista moves a little down the hallway. "I think I was wrong about you. You can't stay here."

"Why?"

"Safety and insurance. Lawsuits."

"I don't understand." I move toward the door. The shadows are long and angular.

"Just come with me." The barista leads me through a network of hallways. We turn left, then right, then right, then right again. The doors aren't so evenly spaced here and as we walk the barista mutters quietly to herself in what sounds like a foreign language. I shiver a little and focus on containing the shivers, on holding them solidly inside. There are no pipes. The doors are all closed. "Go," the barista says. She points to a door at the end of the hallway, the word exit lighted above it.

"Thanks," I say. "I mean that customer thing." I watch the

barista over my shoulder. "Where's this door go?"

"I have to go back to work. Please just go okay?"

I open the door.

I step outside.

FIFTY-SIX

"Don't you want something? Isn't that why you called?" Grandfather said.

I was at college. I pulled my blankets tightly to me. "No." My bedroom was dark and cold and a breeze filtered through the open window. Outside was dark and clear.

"No? Called for no reason then?"

The voice was quiet and static-y and each word, I knew, was a series of beginnings and endings with interruptions and what was missing were the middle-sounds and these middle-sounds were the sounds I wanted and why I listened so carefully then. A voice is a something, I thought but the thought wouldn't go anywhere and I abandoned it. I wanted suddenly to touch and hold the voice, to choke the voice for a while until the voice became something else. "You're wrong," I said.

"I'm sorry."

"Don't be," I said. "Talk about something."

"Okay."

"Okay?"

"Are you eating healthy?" There was a short pause. "Have you rescued any squirrels?"

"No and no. I eat squirrels. I roast them after I catch them with little strings."

"You tie them down?"

"Of course," I said. "That's how I torture them."

"With toothpicks?"

"For the eyes. And with salt, old razor-blades. You know, like grade-school."

"Of course."

I chuckled a little and Grandfather chuckled and we chuckled together.

"Go to the grocery-store."

"What?"

"Tomorrow morning," Grandfather said. "Go to the grocery-store, for groceries. It's important."

"What for?"

"Toothpicks. You'll need more of them. And charcoal."

I laughed.

"Sometimes toothpicks are the only way to survive. Trust me. I lived off them, in New Mexico. I manufactured them in Lisbon. There were squirrels everywhere."

"Pin the eyes back?"

"Pin them back properly," he answered. "Light the little fuckers on fire."

FIFTY-SEVEN

"Hello," I say into my cell-phone.

"Where are you?" It's Merna.

"Somewhere?"

"I need you. We have to plan."

"I don't understand." I begin to walk. My feet slide a little in the snow.

"Grandma won't leave the bedroom."

"Okay."

"So you're coming?"

"I'll try."

"Please," Merna says. "Please?"

I put my cell-phone away. I'm walking. I'm here, I think. I think it again. The sky's gray and very nearby. I imagine my head piercing it. The sky a parking-lot. A mountain-peak. I imagine a thousand blankets and a dim little fire, a flag fluttering above us. I try to imagine Merna's face but Merna's face is not a face.

"Watch where you're going," a person says. The person's face is mostly an open mouth.

"Sorry."

"Aren't we all?"

"Yes," I say.

There's a low gray car.

"Do you need a ride?" a voice says.

"Okay."

There's a body and the body's wide and fat.

"Get in," the voice says.

A door opens.

I step in.

"Can you take me home?"

"Can you take me home?"

The car moves along the road very slowly and I can hear the low packing of snow. My seat feels soft and I'm soft and the air's warm and thick and as I breathe the warm thick air my lungs expand and contract and my lungs process air and oxygen and push warm thick oxygen-molecules through my blood. I think about and imagine my blood and all at once feel that blood and oxygen's pointless, machine-like, painful, and I imagine my blood slowly drained from my body or pumped and suctioned with straws and then bottled and labeled and refrigerated. What would that blood do? Would Bill Murray know? Slumped over the fallen cherry trees. Face in hands.

"So you're here," the voice says. "Car number-two. Nice, huh? My car. Clean it two, three times a day. Vacuum. Wipe down the seats. Feel clean to you? Do you like it?"

"It's nice."

"Just nice?"

"It's nice."

"Fucking perfect."

"Okay."

"Listen to this stereo-system."

I listen.

"Plays CDs, MP3s, the radio, really anything. Satellite-radio. DVDs. I have a sun-roof. Can talk on my cell-phone through the steering-wheel. Call anyone from here without dialing. Watch this: call 'mirror-head', that's my code-name for home. Clever, huh?" There's a ringing followed by an answering-machine. "See," the voice says. "Digital-quality sound. Fucking perfect. Car could be a home—I think of it as my mobile-fortress. Stop. Set up anywhere. New home. Take over, find the mayor, kill the mayor. Become the mayor."

"What would you do if my arm fell off?"

"This car, fucking perfect."

"If right now my head sort of fell off and rolled on the floor and there was blood everywhere and maybe outside tiny boys and girls were pointing and screaming and the blood was on the windshield so you couldn't see, and maybe blood pooling on the seat and floor? What would you do then? Call an ambulance? Panic? Put my head in a tree?"

"Huh? Did I show you the drink-holder?" A button is pushed. From the center-console drink-holders slowly unfold. "Do you have a drink, to put in the drink-holder so I can show you? Or even something cylindrical?"

"No." I imagine the drink-holder full of blood. "What about the blood?"

Outside an elderly man's lying calmly in the snow, blocking the sidewalk. I imagine he's very cold, hibernating, conserving energy. That his heart has slowed, or stopped. That it will start again, in my hand maybe. If I kneel next to him and remove it. I imagine the man in a small white cave, then next to a white lake, then vacationing in Hawaii. In each place the man's lying quietly on the ground, blocking the sidewalk. Passersby step over the man and the man doesn't move but maybe smiles, and each passerby steps carefully over him, doesn't brush him with feet or parcels or even long overcoats. The man's untouchable maybe, protected by a force-field and it's this kind of force-field I want.

"Force-field," I say.

"You like the drink-holder right? I mean it's a clever device. Imagine the time and engineering that went into it. Probably a team of like six engineers. Eighty-thousand dollars a year and testing high-density plastics and hydraulic-devices or I don't know, pneumatic or something."

"It's very nice."

"Very nice?" the voice repeats, quietly. "Very nice?"

I think about energy-conservation. Would it be better to remain motionless, to find a cozy, unimportant space and remain there, unmovable?

"Very nice..." the voice says.

I picture myself in a dark closed-off corner or crawlspace, buried in a box with a flashlight.

"I could be that cup-holder," I say. "It's well-designed because of how it remains out of sight and invisible, energy-efficient. People should be that way. Out of sight, invisible, energy-efficient."

"What the fuck are you talking about?"

"Isn't it evil or sinful to move around so much like people do and to take up so much space and keep other people and animals and plants from using that space? Like a space monopoly? And then using energy and eating food and burning things like fuels and calories or stopping rivers or splitting atoms or whatever. It's like saying we're better and more important and worthy of resource control. I want a little cocoon instead. I could stay in the cocoon, sort of fetal-positioned, quietly remain there until I die."

"Hmm."

"Everyone could have a personal-cocoon, a small licensed space to remain within and then people could be stacked maybe all together on one island like Cuba or underwater or even in a deep hole somewhere like Chernobyl maybe. Lisbon. New Mexico."

"I don't know."

I close my eyes.

"I'm glad you came in my car. It's almost new, and I waxed it today. This morning actually. Couldn't sleep so went directly to the garage and waxed and waxed and vacuumed the car."

"You're taking me home right?"

"Of course."

The voice concentrates on the road. The hands are pudgy and pale and the fingernails are dirty and long and the long dirty fingernails tap the steering-wheel rhythmically but in a frighteningly un-patterned way.

"Listen," the voice says. "You respect me right. I mean, are you worried about before, at Denny's? The dog. Just a silly joke, you know?"

"No."

"Anyway it's just guys and boredom and girls."

"My grandfather died."

"And it was weird anyway because I like dogs actually. And I like Todd a lot. And you too. And Merna. I like people and animals actually."

"I'm going home."

"Lisbon's a good place right? No fighting in Lisbon? No dogs, probably."

I don't answer and gradually the car becomes thin and shadowy so I squint and lean against the window which is cold and smooth. But not really smooth, I think. There are miniature imperfections, cracks or craters, fissures, and especially faces and skin and glass, and glass's a liquid and skin, faces are liquids also, everything is liquid, and all liquids move uncontrollably, reshape and reform themselves, and really every molecule or atom or smaller than that even, every electron or gluon, every vibrating string, is alone and random, operating only in its best interest which is unpredictable and everything's the same and people are just a trillion-billion-billion pieces of something else.

FIFTY-EIGHT

"Why aren't you here yet?"

"I'm coming." Outside the car the sky's dark and gray. I hold my hand over my phone and whisper to the driver, "Where are we?"

"Somewhere."

"I'm almost there," I say into the phone. "I'm somewhere."

"This isn't fucking funny."

"I know," I say. But it is funny, I think. "I'm in a car and the car's moving and the car will move to the house and I'll get out of the car and help. I promise. Because you're my sister and sisters help sisters and I want to help you and it's like when I was ten and we were watching television."

"We were watching television?"

"Yes, television, in the basement and it was very late and we were very tired."

"We helped each other?"

"Of course. We were alone and in the basement and the television played television-shows and it was very dark and cold and outside it was also dark and cold and there was no person anywhere except you and me in the basement watching television."

"What did we do?"

"I don't know."

Merna's silent for a moment.

"I mean how did we help each other?"

"We were very alone but we were together when it was cold probably."

"How did that help?"

"After that we lived with our grandparents. Before, with the television, we were somewhere else and alone and logic probably would tell us that we should split up to survive or something. I was ten after all, or twelve, I don't know. I should've gone to look for berries or video-game-arcades or something and you were older and calm and you might've gone to a friend's house and left me in the basement with the television and I would've been alone and friendless and would have stayed there until I starved probably."

"Are you sure? I think I did leave."

"No, you didn't leave."

"I could've left. Maybe you forgot. Maybe I intended to leave. Maybe I was outside and left a mannequin or pillows or something, a pretend-me, on the couch."

"No, you stayed and we went to the grocery-store and together we stole candy-bars and chocolate-milk and bananas and then outside behind the grocery-store we ate what we stole and we sat awhile."

"I don't remember that at all."

I'm silent and Merna's silent.

The car moves slowly and I think about the car moving and I wonder if the car's pushing my body or pulling my body or even carrying my body and if my body's willing to be pushed or pulled or carried and I wonder if my body controls my body or my brain.

"You done talking?" the voice says. "There're other car-features I want to show you. Trunk-release-lever, keyless-locks, power-windows, other things. Electric-seat-recliner. ABS breaks. I love power-windows the most. Very clever. Important. Engineered and crafted and human-made. Only humans could make power-windows."

I don't answer.

"Are you there?" Merna asks. "Are you still coming?"

"Yes."

"For example, a bear or monkey or dog, couldn't make power-windows."

"Because Noah can't come and Grandma's crying and lying on the floor now and she won't move or eat or drink. I tried to give her water and she'll only stare at the ceiling or me."

"I mean, give your average mammal power-tools and it'll probably just mutilate itself."

"I don't know what to do," I say.

"She could dehydrate. How do you tell if someone's dehydrating?"

"Bloody fur or claws, antlers or something. Give a deer power-tools. A duck!"

"I don't know."

"I think I remember now," Merna says.

"Cartoons are ridiculous with bears flying airplanes or driving. Or with guns."

"What?" I feel confused and tired.

"It wasn't the basement and there was no television. We were on a boat. On the deck and you were maybe thirteen or fourteen and we were near the stern, near the gunwale and it was dark and the waves were very tall."

"I'm not sure," I say.

"The waves were very tall and dark and with foam."

"Sort of immoral. Builds up expectations for animals. Then you go to the zoo."

"If you say so," I say.

"There was a boat and other boats and a bay and we were on the boat on top of a dark wave with foam."

"I," I say. I don't know what to say. "Can people dehydrate in the sea?"

"You don't remember the wave?"

"Monkey'd crash an airplane in two seconds. Bear'd probably fly into a mountain. Kill crew and passengers. Explosion."

"I don't know," I answer.

"We were frightened and the boat was moving, I think."

I try to remember but I don't know how to remember or even how to try to remember.

"Bear massacre. Bear destruction? Animal annihilation?"

"There was a boat," Merna says. Merna's voice's long and raw and certain and I want my voice to sound certain and raw but it never will.

"I'm coming," I say. "I'm almost home."

FIFTY-NINE

"Want to see the cup-holder again?"

I shake my head.

"Okay..."

We're near the ice arena and the snow's thick. I think about the dog and ice-skates and the zamboni and smooth wet ice and driving the zamboni through a wall or car or driving the car through the ice arena windows and out onto the ice and then bouncing from wall to wall like bumper-cars or something.

"What about the bears and monkeys? You think about them?"

"What?"

"Bears and monkeys? Maybe armed. Plastic-explosives. Terrorist animals, at the mall."

"I don't know."

"Can they fly airplanes? Can they stab dogs? Can they eviscerate cashiers?"

I don't answer.

"Don't you wonder? Like, animal apocalypse. Why no revolt? This is important. You need to answer. Are humans better? Are we at war with the animal kingdom? Should we go to the zoo and murder like bears or penguins? Stab the penguins and then the orangutans, pile their corpses somewhere, roast them or something. Does it matter or what?"

"Okay," I say. "That's all fine."

"What do you mean? Are you for or against animal-slaughter and barbeque? I couldn't sleep last night and I thought about this a lot. It's the cartoons, I think. It's a war or something. So what the fuck do you mean?"

"All of it," I say. "It's fine. It doesn't matter. Animals or no animals. It's exactly the same."

"What's to stop me from killing everything that moves? Shouldn't I?"

The car moves slowly around a broad corner and up a low hill.

"Where are you going?" I ask.

"Just need a second."

"I'm supposed to go home."

"I know. Have to stop a second. An errand. Think about the animals and this war thing I was talking about."

We're in the ice arena parking-lot. The car stops.

"What now?" I say.

"Get out."

SIXTY

"I have to go," I say. I'm standing in the ice arena parking-lot and my feet are buried in snow and ice and my feet are cold and thin and I fear that if I move my feet my feet will shatter slowly and leave me wobblingly standing on ankle-stumps and dark frozen blood. "What are we doing here?"

"Necromancy."

"What?"

"The dog. Nothing."

"Hmm."

"Like necro-surgery with chemicals and shit," the voice says. It moves. "I've got nitrogen and, nuclear salts...anyway, I'm lying. Dog's dead. Dead-dog and buried. Time to revitalize the security-guard."

"I have to go home."

"Just a second. Todd's coming. Todd's meeting us here."

"Who's Todd?"

"Erik."

In my brain Erik's a faceless shape in a shapeless fog and there's a mouth and the mouth's moving so I listen for words but there are no words and only a gray shapeless face and a gigantic mechanical mouth opening and closing.

"Besides, promised the security-guard he could fuck you."

"I don't fuck security-guards."

"Just this once," the voice says. "In the ass."

"I don't have time for this. Merna's waiting," I say. "Merna needs me."

"She'll be fine. Just a few minutes. We promised the security-guard, okay. Part of the deal."

"I don't care."

"Don't you care about my good word?"

"Have to help plan a funeral."

"Don't make me your fucking liar. I promised, okay. Liars should be mutilated, randomly, with fire-axes or something. With pole-axes."

I begin walking. I walk in a circle. I circle the voice and the car. My feet form a narrow rut and don't shatter and slowly my feet warm until the warmth's almost unbearable and I wonder why my feet aren't melting the snow and dissolving the snow and slowly turning the snow into steam because, I think, my feet are steam-engines, steam-engines, steam-shovels, my feet are steam-shovels. I picture my feet as steam-shovels with nothing to shovel. The car's angle-parked and low and the voice's leaning against the car and above us the sky's low and very nearby and the parking-lot's snow-covered and unrecognizable as a parking-lot and distantly the ice arena waits with wide reflective windows. Near the largest window stands a gray figure and the figure's arms are raised and immobile with shadowy spread-fingered hands.

"Come on," the voice says.

"Merna needs me," I say. "I want to go home. I want to see Merna."

"It's just an errand. Five minutes. Maybe ten. Grandpa's not going anywhere."

We walk narrowly and at angles and as I watch the snowy ground our progress is slow and inefficient, but when I look up I see we're approaching the gray figure quickly and mechanically so the figure looms large and shadowy before the windows.

"Why?" I say aloud.

"What?"

My brain tries to answer but my mouth's silent. Why follow? I think. I push and prod my brain but it stops. There are no answers and no questions. My cold feet in the snow-rut. The brown dead snow. We stand before the figure. The figure's face is a gigantic mouth and the mouth's open and wide with a wide row of thin shiny teeth.

"Back to the ice-palace," the figure says.

"Let's go inside," the voice says.

I watch them.

"Okay, I have to go now," I say.

My cell-phone plays a little song.

"That's Merna and I have to leave but it's good seeing you and stuff."

"Just grab her arm," the voice says. "I'll grab the other arm."

"Do it carefully," the figure says. "Don't bruise the arm."

"I'll call you later maybe. We'll go out for chocolate cake or something. See a movie."

"Get the door."

"I have your phone-numbers already in my cell-phone, probably. Or you could write them down for me. I probably have a pad you could write your numbers on, if you have a pen or pencil, or I might have a pencil in my pocket."

"Be quiet," the voice says. "Can't concentrate."

The door opens.

"I'll get the lights," the figure says.

"You could take me home now. Just you and me."

"Be quiet. No time for that." The voice locks the door behind us.

"What about Lisbon, what about the dog?"

"Sshhh."

I try to move my arm but the voice holds it stiffly in place.

"My arm hurts. What if my arm falls off or something? You don't want to be responsible for that? You'd be holding it. Detached arm. Bleeding."

"Shut the fuck up."

"We could go together and rob banks or something. You could hang out with my grandmother and Merna, watch TV. Something, something. We could do something, something."

The lights above the ice flicker and are bright and thin and fluorescent. All else is dark. The figure returns. The figure's arms are long and narrow and now jacket-less and hairy and the arms are crossed over the figure's chest. As he approaches, the arms slowly unfold and release the fingers and the fingers encircle my arm.

"Let's go," the figure says.

"To the ice?" the voice asks.

"Yes, to the ice."

"Do you have the plan?"

The figure pats its pocket. "Of course."

"Can I see the plan? I need to call and tell Merna the plan because Merna deserves to know the plan and really she's part of the plan because Merna was here earlier and Merna tried to save the dog and took us to the hospital and to Noah who was the doctor."

"Try and be quiet."

I watch them and they become mirrored images of one another. But one's very fat and wide with a small shaky head and pudgy dirty hands, and the other's very thin and long with strangely angled limbs so that it seems impossible that the pair could be mirrored images of one another, but they are somehow.

"Twinned," I say aloud.

"Just be quiet."

My cell-phone ring-tone plays a little song.

"I have to answer this," I say.

I turn on my cell-phone.

"Hello," I say.

"Listen—"

The figure takes my cell-phone and turns off my cell-phone and places the cell-phone carefully in its pocket.

"No calls. Not in the plan."

"Let me see the plan."

"She wants to see the plan," the voice says.

"Should we show her the plan?"

"I don't know, she might laugh."

The figure pats its horizontally-striped breast-pocket and the breast-pocket's bulging and the stripes are thin and gray.

"What could we do if she laughs?"

I imagine myself as a thin gray stripe.

"She might cry, or try to run."

"I don't want to chase her," the figure says.

"I don't want to chase her either."

"Then we can't show her the plan, can we?"

"No, that'd be disaster."

There's a pause.

"You can't see the plan right now. But later, maybe, I'll give it to you. I'll put it in your pocket."

"We can't have you laughing because if you laughed I'd cry and then there'd be laughing and crying, or you might cry and then there'd by crying and crying or crying and laughing, all at the same time."

"We can't have that."

"No, we can't."

"Come with us."

"Yes, come."

They walk me forward. The ice's ahead and there's a gate and the gate's ajar and wide and the ice beyond's white and rough and dull. Our movement's smooth and conjoined and for a moment I feel like a miniature chrome-sprocket. I picture the chrome-sprocket and it's spinning and clicking and I'm the clicking and I am clicking and there's clicking because something clicks. My arms are numb. As we approach the gate, our speed increases until the gate's before me and I'm in the gate and I'm moving upward and sideways and my body's twisting and I want suddenly to see my body from a distance and enjoy the movements of the body as it searches slowly for balance, but all I see is ice and a blurred light and I'm airborne and falling until the ice is all there is and the ice's holding me. I can't say anything. My lungs are empty. I push until I stop. When I stop, I don't move.

I don't have to move, I think.

I should be motionless and close my eyes, I think.

I close them. I hold them closed.

SIXTY-ONE

If I could sit with Grandfather I would say, "We should steal like twenty-five llamas, set them free downtown. Or tether the llamas to police-cars and egg the police-cars, then steal potted-plants from cemeteries and business parks."

"Why," Grandfather might ask.

"I've always wanted to steal potted-plants."

If I said the same things to Merna, Merna would say, "That's illegal."

"I know," I might say. "But what's 'illegal' mean anyway?"

Grandmother might say, "Llamas are filthy animals and they smell bad."

"You smell bad," I'd answer.

If we rode a passenger-train, we'd dine in the dining-car with space-aliens and sit quietly with the space-aliens and discuss politics. "Are you some kind of commie-liberal," I might ask the space-alien. Grandfather would laugh

"What's a 'commie-liberal'?" the space-alien would ask because the space-alien's planet's has no political-parties.

"Do you like to share your resources and labor and things with other space-aliens so that all space-aliens have basically the same things and work the same amount?" I'd say.

"What are 'things' and 'work'?"

This is where we'd grow frustrated and stab the space-aliens with our steak-knives, then drop the space-alien-bodies from the back of the train where they would tumble over dusty train-tracks and bounce a little until they were gone.

"How many eyes do they have?" Grandfather would ask.

"They don't have eyes."

"Then how do they see?" Grandfather would act perplexed.

"With belly-buttons. They have belly-button x-ray machines in their belly-buttons."

"And who will bury their bodies?"

"The government," I would answer. "To hide the space-aliens from us, but only after removing the x-ray machines, experimenting with the x-ray machines, possibly dissecting the space-aliens with scalpels and lasers maybe."

"I'd put them in a museum," Grandfather might answer. "Stuff them taxidermically and model the space-aliens in life-like positions. Cooking. Piloting space-crafts." Grandfather would chuckle and stand very tall and watch the horizon. "I'd leave the steak-knives in their alien-chests and display the aliens in a darkened room and charge a twenty-dollar entry-fee." Then we'd all agree for a while and imagine the space-alien-museum and drink chocolate-milk in a parking-lot on Mount Everest near a little campfire and the sky would be clear and distant and thick.

SIXTY-TWO

"Kick her," someone says. "Kick her stupid face."

"Don't move," I say. My eyes are closed.

"Quiet."

I'm curled and still and my body's a soft round ball. My body spins. There's blood on my face probably and blood on other places and the blood's warm.

"My name's fucking Todd."

I slide or my body slides. I think, I'm sliding.

"That's funny. Do it again."

Laughing.

"No, you."

There's silence. Face, I think.

"Cut her fucking fingers off."

"What?"

"Scissors or shears or something."

"Toes, maybe."

I cover my head with my arms and from every side I feel sudden sharp blows or something else that has no name so that each part of my body curls into itself, so that each part of my body is separate and isolated. There's a hand and other hands and tearing and I'm shirtless maybe and cold or my body's cold and shivering but separately in separate parts and I'm dragged awhile. Something slowly removes my hair.

Laughing.

"Bitch."

"Grab pants. Pants grab."

"Choke with pants."

Laughing.

"Choke."

"Funny word."

"Choke, choke."

Laughing.

"Choke, choke."

I'm naked or feel naked or somehow my isolated parts are naked or unclothed or cold and wet and vibrating or shaking strangely so I am detached and nervous and in my brain there's only the image of trembling fingers. My body feels the ice and holds itself in a ball and the body shivers except for where warm blood traces it.

"Cut the fucking nipple off."

I think about Merna for a while. Pregnant, I think. I'm not and never will be pregnant. I stop. I want to separate into isolated self-sufficient pieces, for the pieces to move to different cities, different countries, independent and brain-less, because brain-less body-parts are efficient or economical or something. I keep my eyes closed and wonder if brains can close too. Or close down, I think. I want suddenly to be home, to lie quietly on the couch, to feel the couch-cushions against my parts until I hide them beneath the couch-cushions or behind the television. But

Lisbon, I think. Body-parts to Lisbon, beneath dumpsters or hidden in churches, cafés or along dark and useless highways. Body-parts as gifts to homeless children. Body-parts as food.

"She's shivering."

"Fuck, that's funny."

I'm a ball.

"Stomp."

"That, do that. Good."

"I'm shivering," I say. "I'm not shivering my body's shivering and my body-parts are shivering and separate and not me and I am not me now but there's something."

"Sshhh. Concentrating here."

"Yes, that."

"Chop the lips, maybe."

Laughing.

Can hardly move.

Speak but muffled. I say, "The body shivers is shivering the body's mine and wet and cold and shivers is shivering or something something I am something now or am now something shivering this body the."

My mouth's moving and talking and I think about my mouth and concentrate on the mouth-movements and mouth-sounds and for a while other things happen.

Then things stop.

SIXTY-THREE

"I am twenty-years-old yesterday," I say aloud. Nobody answers. I'm in a narrow room with white walls and thin white venetian-blinds. Wedges of sun work through the blind slats and line the wall behind me with shadows that widen at their ends. There are two empty beds. My bed's soft and comfortable and I lie unmovingly in it because I'm not moving and won't move and will not be moved. It's very quiet. There's a television but it's distant and gray. The remote-control sits on a thick plastic tray-table next to my bed but I ignore the remote and the table so they don't exist. "I don't have anything to say," I say. There's a door. The door opens. It's Merna. Merna's crying. "Are you okay?" I ask. "What happened?"

"I called the police."

"You'll be okay. We'll watch television." I don't know why I say this. "Turn on the television and we'll watch it. There'll be lots to watch and we'll watch together and we can watch and be the watchers. Like the news and sitcoms. Like People's Court and commercials for bar-soap and maybe The Travel Channel."

"What will you say?"

"You'll watch with me won't you?"

"When the police come you'll have to say something so they can write a report."

"I'll watch you Merna. I can watch you, can't I?"

"Who were they? What'd they want?"

"Pretty Merna."

"I'll stab something."

I hum for a while and stare at the ceiling.

"Don't you want to say something? Aren't you concerned about the police-report? Accuracy? You should make notes or something. Get it all down."

I shake my head.

"Aren't you angry?"

"No, Merna. I'm not and never have been angry."

There's a silence.

"No reason to be angry," I say. "No reason to be anything ever at all."

Others enter the room through the door and they are gray men and women and the gray men and women sit along the far wall near the television and a tiny brown potted-fern. The gray men and women talk quietly to each other and in little black notepads they produce from large pants-pockets, the gray men and women write long and hasty notations. I listen for the whispers but the whispers are quiet and low and covered by cupped-hands so I lie back in my soft and comfortable bed and think about Merna who has walked into the white hallway and who now paces in front of the still-open door and talks into her cell-phone. I look at my hand and my hand's cold.

"Excuse me," I say.

"Yes," a woman says. She cups her hand over her mouth and

whispers something to her colleagues. When she receives an answer, she says, "Can I be of assistance?"

"Yes you can."

"How may we be of assistance?" another woman asks.

"We want to be helpful," a man says.

"Do you need anything?" a different man asks. "We can fluff pillows or bring new blankets or turn on the television. We could bring you a soda or something. Do you like Pepsi-cola?"

"I don't want any of that."

"Well, what do you want?" the first woman asks.

"You must want something," a man says.

"Does she want money or what?" the woman says. "Everybody wants a little money."

I don't answer.

"Money to buy things," the woman says. "You could buy chocolate-cake or ice cream."

"How about a beach-ball?" the man says to the woman.

"Would you like a beach-ball?" the woman asks.

The man watches his hands. "People can toss a beach-ball back and forth as a game. It's fun. You could toss a beach-ball with your sister and think about the beach and the ocean and sitting on the beach and tossing beach-balls and watching the limitless ocean. You'd like that, wouldn't you?"

"The ocean?" I shake my head. "I don't know," I say.

"She doesn't know," a man says.

"She doesn't know," a woman says. "What does she know? What

does a person know?"

"What do you know?" the other woman says.

Merna's outside the door and speaking into her cell-phone and I want suddenly to be Merna's cell-phone and for Merna to speak into me. To be an object, I think, is probably the most satisfying occupation.

"She didn't answer," a man says. He makes a note.

"Why didn't you answer?" a woman asks. "Did you understand the question? You speak English, don't you?"

I nod.

"She speaks English!"

"Yes."

"She does."

"Ask her something."

"Yes, ask her something."

"Why are you here?"

"Where's here?"

The men and women look at other men and women. "This is a hospital."

"I'm tired," I say. "I'm here because I'm tired and because I am twenty-years-old yesterday."

The gray men and women make many notes, and for a while there's only the sound of note-taking. Merna reenters the room and sits lightly at the end of my soft and comfortable bed.

"Noah's coming later," Merna says. "Grandma and Noah'll come together."

I don't answer. I touch Merna with my foot and Merna's body's soft and solid and very nearby so I rest my foot against the body and imagine the body as my body and so that every body's one body and connected somehow and quiet.

"Do you speak English?" a man asks Merna.

"Yes, please. Do you?" a woman asks.

"Yes," Merna says.

"She speaks English!" a woman says.

"Tell us about her," a man says.

"Please," the other man says.

"What does she know?" the woman asks.

"Neither of us know anything ever at all," Merna says.

"Yes," I say. "That's exactly it."

SIXTY-FOUR

There's a doctor. The doctor holds a silver clipboard. The doctor's face is narrow and wrinkled and the wrinkles are extensive and interconnecting and I imagine tracing the wrinkles with my pinky-finger but my pinky-finger's too large and even in my brain I fail.

"How are we today?" the doctor asks. "Hmm," the doctor says. The doctor's red-painted fingernails tap the clipboard. "We'll fix you up," the doctor says.

"I'm okay," I say. "I probably don't need to be fixed. Probably."

"Yes," the doctor says. "I see." The doctor makes a notation. "I have something to tell you: pancreatic-cancer's really terrible." The doctor watches me. "Adenocarcinoma. Ninety-nine-percent of victims die within five years, painfully. Jaundice, blood clots, depression." The doctor chuckles. "Good thing you were only attacked."

"Hmm," I say.

"That's from my humor-model. I'm a part-time humorologist. What do you think?"

I don't answer.

"Emotional tension, then release. That's the theory. But you're not laughing...I don't know. Doesn't always work, I guess."

"Can I go today?"

"Defenestration?"

"What?"

The doctor makes a note. "You can go whenever you want."

I consider this. "Where should I go?"

"Wherever you want."

"Where do people go?"

"Home, theme-parks, New Mexico."

"Hmm."

"Video-game arcades, Mount Rainier, inside submarines."

"Where would you go if you could go somewhere?" I watch the doctor.

"I'd disappear."

"Disappear?"

"I'd disappear everyday and change and be a new person in a new somewhere." The doctor sets her clipboard down. "You know, with costumes and stuff."

SIXTY-FIVE

Noah's car's cold and soft and lined everywhere with brown leather. Merna sits in the front-passenger-seat. My step-grand-mother sleeps softly beside me in back. The sky's bright and cold and the sun warms me through the car-window so I lean my face against the window and it's cold and hard. Noah parks in the driveway. "Thank you for the ride," I say.

"You're welcome."

"Let's go inside," Merna says.

"Okay." I wake my step-grand-mother. "Did you finish the funeral?" I ask Merna.

"What do you mean?" Merna unlocks the door and we step inside.

"For Grandpa."

"No," Merna says. "He's still in bed. Didn't want to move him."

"Oh."

"We should make some calls."

"Who do we call?"

"I don't know, the police, funeral parlors, somebody."

Noah sits on the kitchen-counter. Step-grand-mother walks to the family-room-couch and lays her body on the couch and slowly closes her eyes.

"What do we do with the body?" I ask. "Noah, you must know."

"I don't know," Noah says. "I'll research it for you." Noah walks out of the kitchen and disappears.

"Let's go upstairs," I say.

"What?"

"Let's see Grandpa."

"I don't think that's a good idea."

"It'll be calming."

"I can't look at him again and you should rest. You shouldn't do anything at all."

"We have to look at it. It's an it now, not a him. You could close your eyes."

Merna watches me and Merna's eyes are very large and round and soft so that I want to touch her eyes but I don't touch her eyes. "But you need to rest, take a shower or something. Lay in bed. I can bring you food or coffee or whatever."

"I'm okay and I want to see Grandpa."

"Okay, fine." Merna walks toward the stairs.

"Thank you."

The hallway's lined with doors and as we pass the doors I touch them and the doors are solid and rough.

Merna opens Grandpa's door. "Okay," she says. "Ready?"

I nod. We go in the bedroom. I reach for the light-switch.

"Don't," Merna says. "No lights."

"Okay." I walk to the side of the bed. Merna walks to the other side of the bed and we watch each other across the bed and across Grandfather's body which is round and long and which rises beneath the blankets very mound-like and still. I lay my hand on the belly. "We need to take it," I say.

"What?"

"The body. We should take it somewhere outside and sunny." I sit on the bed. "We should put it in the car and drive it somewhere and take care of it ourselves."

"You can't do that."

"It's our grandfather."

"There are laws."

I watch Merna and Merna watches me. "We could take it to Lisbon. Grandpa would like that. We could ship it maybe. Or drive it to the sea and steal a boat and drive the boat to Lisbon. We could preserve the body in a box with ice or nitrogen or I don't know and take the body somewhere. It's our duty, isn't it? He's our grandfather not somebody else's and his body's dead and done or something and our body's also will be dead and done one day and would we want our body's given to the government or whatever or burned and buried quietly in some expensive grave-plot?"

"He's dead," Merna says. Her voice's low and warble-y.

"I want the body and to care for the body and take the body carefully to Lisbon or somewhere like Kansas."

"I'll call the police."

I don't answer.

"I'll tell Grandma and Noah. I'll tell everybody."

"It doesn't matter."

Merna walks to the doorway. "You wouldn't want them to know

anyway. It'll be a funeral and okay. You're just panicking or something."

Merna leaves, shutting the door behind her. I move my body closer to Grandfather's body and the body's cold and solid and I touch the belly and the face and carefully close the mouth and eyes. I watch the face and face doesn't move. The body doesn't move and the room temperature doesn't change. There's no sound and I don't think or want anything. I watch the digital-clock. I slowly lie next to Grandfather. I look at the body. I close my eyes.

SIXTY-SIX

Night.

Merna, Step-grand-mother, Noah asleep.

My bedroom's still and gray and I sit grayly on the floor.

"Wake and funeral tomorrow," I say.

In my brain the body remains silent and immovable in bed and alone with no suit and no make-up and no expression on its gray face. Body, I think. It. I close my eyes and the body's in my brain and I think about my body, my body unmoving and undressed and silent and in my mind I place my body next to Grandfather's so there are two unmoving bodies. In the corner of my bedroom stands the tall thin man, his hands flat on perpendicular walls. "This," the man says. He shows me his hand and his hand's narrow with long thin fingers and an unlined palm.

"Now," I say.

"This?" he says.

"Shut up," I say. I'm bored with the man so I put him away. When I put the man away, he reappears. "You're not here," I say. "You're not a you," I say. "I'm bored, okay." I blink for a while. "I'm sorry. I was rude." I stand and walk quietly into Grandfather's bedroom and in the darkness stand next to Grandfather's body. I close my eyes and carefully place my hand on Grandfather's stomach.

253

In the corner of the bedroom stands the tall thin man, his hands flat on perpendicular walls. "This?" he says.

"Yes," I say. I don't know why I say that. "I'm sorry."

"Keys?"

"Yes," I say.

I take the keys from Grandfather's dresser and place them in my pocket.

I squat and roll the body onto my shoulder, the arms of it sliding along my back. I stand and lift and consider the weights of bodies, the lightness of them. I carry the body through the still-open door, down the stairs slowly and quietly, along the long hallway, and carefully down into the garage. I concentrate on each step and watch the floor in front of me. I keep my body low, my back straight, my knees bent.

"I wrote a lifting-technique manual," I imagine Grandfather saying. "Drew diagrams, on a trek through the Pyrenees. Patented the instructions in Madrid. Sold the patents in Marseilles. Became a millionaire and lost the millions at a craps table in Borneo."

"Did you journey with llamas?"

"Yes, with llamas. Spanish llamas. Hairy and with big swollen teats. Then gambled with the Portuguese."

I lay the body on the hood of the Cadillac where it shifts and swings and slides, the head lolling then stopping. I open the Cadillac and move the body onto the backseat. I turn off my cell-phone and start the Cadillac. I carefully lower the power-windows. I'm humming. I put the Cadillac in reverse.

"Okay," I say aloud. "Okay."

"Yes," I say. "Drive the car," I say.

I drive the car.

It's dark and there's snow and the air's cold on my face but I drive the Cadillac and the Cadillac's driving and being driven and moving quickly from streetlight to streetlight and the Cadillac's large and hardly controlled and I know I can't control the Cadillac but can only guide it so I guide the Cadillac and only when the Cadillac slides do I close my eyes.

"This," I say.

I'm smiling.

"Pyrenees," I say. "Lisbon."

I think about turning on my cell-phone and calling Merna.

No, I think. I can't and won't call any person.

The lights are spaced further apart until there are only the Cadillac's headlights and the dash-lights and I watch the dash-lights and they're bright and solid and I'm between the dash-lights and cold and awake.

"This," I say.

I don't know what I mean because I don't know anything which is perfect and planned. I think about something for a while but I forget what it is and think about other things.

At the rest stop I place a blanket over Grandfather's body. There are no cars and the bathroom's slanted and backlighted. The sky's distant and clouded and dark.

"Let me know if there's anything you need," I say to myself.

I'm looking at the blanket.

"I don't need things."

I sit in the Cadillac and think about the ocean. There's a digital-clock in the dash and I watch the clock for a while. Then I don't.